Riley's Revival

New Beginnings

Written By:

K.C. Hart

ISBN 9781729605639

Library Congress Number 1-8203887671

CreateSpace Independent Publishing Platform (October 25, 2019)

Any references made to historical events, real people, or real places are used fictitiously. Names, characters and places are the product of the author's imagination.

Front Cover Image by K.C. Hart and Jared Hart

Back Cover Image by K.C. Hart

Note from the author...

I have spent many years thinking about ways to help children, especially children whose parents are in the military deal with some of the struggles and challenges they face in everyday life. Through the life of Riley, I hope that this book helps kids and families deal with some of the challenges they face.

I want to thank everyone who helped me write and edit this book. Cheryl Nunes and David Spector, your time and energy put into editing this book was amazing and I greatly appreciate it.

Paul Newman for your ideas on how to reach many people as I can with this book.

Ryan Cunningham for your input and descriptions of different jobs in the Air Force.

My husband, Jared Hart, for putting up with my long hours of writing and supporting me each step of the way.

All my friends and family for giving me their input on how they handle different challenges that military families face.

My parents for bringing me up to always look to Him as my first love and to not stray from that.

Dedication

This book is dedicated to my dear friend, Rachelle Kelly, who taught me to live life to its fullest, to be gracious and kind to those you meet and to dance like you never have danced before. Rest in peace, my friend. May God hold you in His loving arms until we meet again.

Introduction

Hi. My name is Riley Tanner, and I'm thirteen years old. Just an ordinary girl, who likes simple things. Horses, basketball and getting into trouble are right up my alley. Well, I really don't like getting into trouble; it just seems to follow me as I'm very curious. I worry a lot and try to fix other people's problems.

My mother, Sarah Tanner and my grandmother, Rose Brown and I all live together. My mom's in the Air Force and we live in a different place pretty much every three years. Our most recent and hopefully final move has taken us to Cape Cod, Massachusetts. My mom got a job at Otis Air Force Base as a crew chief. It's a sweet job and she's good at what she does. I'm an only child and never met my Dad. My Dad is a mystery to me, as my mom doesn't talk about him and it drives me crazy. What I do know is that he was in the Marines Corps and died in combat.

My new home is awesome cause we're right down the street from the beach and canal. The outdoors is my favorite place to be, so I will fit in great here. Buckle up and get ready because you are in for a ride as I tell you the story of my life and take you on some awesome adventures!

Chapter One

Summer had come and gone and I couldn't believe that school was already here. Days of having fun with Mom and Grandma were over. Our trip to Disney World was awesome, especially seeing Goofy, my favorite character. I really liked seeing my family too. My aunts, uncles and all my cousins had barbeques on the beach and played volleyball. I even learned what a clam bake was and how to play beach volleyball. Thinking back to those summer days, I can smell the salty ocean water and taste the delicious lobster dipped in butter. I'll never forget the feel of the sand between my toes. It reminded me of sandpaper but with a smooth and relaxing feeling as if someone was giving me a massage while getting a pedicure. *Man, would I love a pedicure right now!*

But those days are over. Now it is time to go back to school, and a new school at that. My days will be filled with reading, writing, math, and tons of homework. I closed my eyes as my mind raced and thought over the many questions that were in my head.

How would I ever survive? Would the other kids like me? Would I be popular or would the other kids make fun of me?

Sometimes, I wish my mom didn't have to get stationed at a new place. Moving, changing schools, and losing the friends that I had made were all things that I hated about starting over. The only good part is that family was nearby so that was cool and would help me get through starting my life over. Mom said we would be here until she retired and that this was the final stop on her military career. I couldn't count how many times we had moved over my thirteen years of life. Staying in one place, where I could make friends and grow up with them, would make me the happiest girl on the planet. Maybe this would be my shot at a normal life.

I bounced the basketball and took a shot from my homemade three-point line.

Playing ball by myself is so boring.

As nervous as I was about school starting, I was excited to meet new friends and hopefully find someone to hang out with. I took one more shot and called it quits. I had to go and get my stuff ready for school before dinner. It was a perfect night to be playing under the street light and I could hear kids off in the distance having fun. The sky was lit up by a light orange and yellow ball that cast a beautiful ray of light over the sky. It was pretty and gave me a warm feeling, as I walked back into the house.

My grandmother's house was huge and right down the street from Sagamore Beach. It was an old colonial style house that had a basement, first floor, second floor and an attic. The paint on the outside was chipping off and it needed to be repainted. The yard needed to be cared for, all two acres of it, but no one seemed to mind the mess. My grandma had my room repainted last year when I visited and it was a pretty shade of yellow with blue trim. I was very surprised that she was willing to part with the wallpaper that had been pasted on many years before my time. Grandma said that this was my mom's room growing up. My mom bought me a blue zebra striped fleece blanket that was very warm since it gets cold in the winter time. I had an air conditioner in my room that made the summer heat a little more bearable. The sun was always coming through the light blue lacey drapes that hung on the windows. It was kind of pretty if you asked me. I found a worn leather Bible and my grandmother's journal in the nightstand. She said to keep them there in case I got bored and wanted to read them. She winked at me when she said it. Don't get me wrong, I like reading the Bible, but this one seemed worn and I didn't want the pages to fall out. I put it in a box under my bed so I wouldn't ruin it. The most interesting part of this room was the stained-glass skylight that lit up the room with awesome colors when the sun came through it. Mom must have loved this room as a kid.

I wish we were talking to each other right now. I would ask her so many questions about her room.

The attic was the only place that I was not allowed to go. My mom and grandma both made a point of making sure I knew this rule and it made me curious. One day I knew I would find out what the big deal was all about. My mom put up a basketball hoop in the driveway so I could practice. Hopefully I would find friends that would want to come over and play ball. Then there was the canal, which has a beautiful lighthouse, a long jetty of rocks, and lots of runners who get their exercise on the flat paved trail. The current is extremely fast and the water is off limits to swimmers but not to fisherman. I love watching the fishermen cast their lines into the current and pull up huge fish. Tall ships and huge barges travel through the waters and I couldn't wait to see them again one day. It was just up the road. I love to run with my mom and ride my bike so this would be perfect.

I was struggling to find the perfect outfit for my first day of school. I wanted to make an impression but not stand out too much. Jeans or workout pants? Shorts or a dress? I wish I didn't have so many choices. My older cousin had just given me a ton of hand-me-downs because we didn't have much money since my mom was a single mom and was in the military. As I mulled over my clothes, I could hear my friend Sally saying, "Riley, just remember to be yourself. People will love you." She was so sad that we weren't going to be in the same class together anymore, never mind the same state. We had promised to text, call, and Facetime when we could. I made a promise to visit every…

"Riley!" I could hear Mom's voice over my music and it pulled me back to reality. I could barely hear my mom over country singer, Carrie Underwood's voice singing "*Jesus, Take the Wheel*" so I turned it down.

"Time for dinner!" Mom called out. I could tell there was a hint of aggravation in her voice. She hated when I played my music loud in the house.

Sweet! I was starving. "Coming, Mom!" I turned Carrie off and pushed my dresser drawer shut, thinking I'll have to pick out my outfit later. I raced downstairs to help set the table.

"Riley, you excited about your first day at school?" My grandmother asked as I pulled the dishes out of the cabinet. Mom looked at me curiously as we had yet to speak about school since we had the fight about moving. I looked at my grandmother and she wrinkled her nose a little bit like she always does when she feels there's a little tension. I know this because I do the same thing and she reminds me of it all the time.

"Yea, I guess, Grandma." I shrugged my shoulders, wrinkled my nose, and added, "I'm a little nervous about meeting new people. I heard they have a good basketball team though. I hope to try out in the fall."

"That sounds like a good idea, Riley." Mom said, raising her eyes. I could hear the excitement in her voice. She seemed very eager for me to get involved.

"I'm going to be working late tomorrow. I have a plane coming at 1900 and the crew and I need to do a complete inspection of it so it can be flown on a mission the next day," mom explained. "Grandma will be here after school and there will be leftovers in the fridge. I'll call after dinner to make sure that you're all set. I'm already excited to hear about your first day. I hope you really enjoy it."

"No problem, Mom." I tried to hide my disappointment and aggravation but my mom always saw right through me. I wish she had a nine to five job where she could be home at night, especially after my first day of school. It was kind of a big deal, but I didn't want mom to feel even more guilty than she already did. "I get it, you have to work. Don't worry, grandma and I will be fine. I'll probably just play basketball in the driveway or go for a walk and meet our new neighbors." I hoped my smile masked my sadness and frustration. *I couldn't believe that the Air Force is again ruining my life with my mom,* I thought. *There's no use dragging up that old wound right now though. Sometimes I wonder if Mom likes working such long and crazy hours. I wonder if she likes being around me.*

"Riley? Did you hear your grandmother?" Mom asked. Both my mother and my grandmother were staring at me with quizzical looks on their faces.

"No, Mom, I didn't. Sorry, Grandma, what did you say?" I'd been too deep in thought to hear my grandmother.

Grandma replied, "I asked what movie would you like to watch tonight?"

I thought for a minute and replied, "How about *The Money Pit*? It's really funny and it would be perfect to watch before my first day of school."

I looked at my mom as she nodded her head in agreement. "Well then, it's settled," Grandma stated.

Dinner conversation then turned to how the day was so beautiful and what our favorite parts of the movie were. My favorite part was when the tub fell through the floor and the character, Tom Hanks, laughed this awesome laugh. I explained to mom and grandma that it always made me laugh so hard I almost peed my pants. Tom Hanks has the facial expressions down pat when it came to laughing and used his whole body in the laugh that made it even better. After dinner finished, we settled in for a night of popcorn and laughs.

Chapter Two

The first day of school wasn't bad at all. Once I got past introducing myself over and over in each class, I began to see what the school and other kids were all about. The design of the school was basically the same as the last school I was in, which made it easy to find things. *I wonder if all base schools are built the same way?* It was in the shape of a square and there were maps on some of the walls to make it easier for new kids like me. The lockers were a dark blue and each had a spin dial lock with a combo. I hoped mine was an easy number to remember. I also secretly wished that my locker was next to someone cool or who would become my best friend over the years. The hallways smelled of fresh paint, which for some weird reason reminded me of the first day of school.

The teachers were nice and students were ok. As soon as I walked into the cafeteria, I could already tell that there were different cliques just like my old school. As I looked around the room, I could see the "geeks" who were doing schoolwork at their table and were wearing glasses and bowties; the "smart" kids who just looked like they were already looking down at me for not looking smart; the "jocks" made up of both girls and boys who were wearing converse sneakers and joggers; and the "snobby" kids who were wearing name brand clothing and texting on their cell phones underneath the table. Having cell phones in school, even at lunch, was a big no in many schools so I didn't want to get in trouble on my first day. I wasn't too keen on sitting with the jocks since I wasn't on the team and didn't know if I would be welcome. *Rather than stepping on any toes, I think I'll just find another table.* I decided to sit down at a table that seemed to be filled with normal kids that didn't fit into a group and hopefully would have good luck there.

"Hey, do you mind if I sit here?" I asked with slight hesitation. My stomach was doing flips because the boy that I was about to sit down next to was kind of cute. *I don't know if this is such a good idea.*

"Sure, go ahead," said the tall, curly brown haired, blue eyed boy. His perfect smile is what really got me and his face was full of freckles that made him look even cuter. He was wearing jeans and a red and black plaid shirt.

"My name is Sebastian. I think we have English together." I was taken back that he was so cute but held my tongue and replied, "I'm Riley. And yes, I have English with Mrs. Tanzy. I spent most of the class just trying to figure out what we were going to be learning. Sorry I didn't notice you." I instantly felt bad but shrugged it off.

"No worries," said Sebastian, smiling. "This is Chloe," he said, pointing to the dark haired, green eyed girl. "She moved here a few years ago and we get along pretty good." He winked at her and she playfully glared at him.

"Hey, Riley. I was the new kid before so feel free to ask me anything at all." She seemed so nice. *I wonder if Sebastian and Chloe are dating. It really wasn't any of my business seeing that we had just met, but it crossed my mind.*

"I was trying to figure out when basketball tryouts were. Either of you know or play on the team by any chance?" I asked. Both shook their heads but pointed to the flyer on the wall. "Ahhh. thank you." I reached up and pulled the flyer down and began to read it. It had all the information and I couldn't wait to show my mom. *Wait, I can't talk to my mom about this because we're arguing. I'll just have to wait. The whole reason I want to try out for a new team is because of her and the stupid Air Force.* I brought myself out of my head and realized I had about two weeks before tryouts so I had time to figure it all out.

"So, Riley," Chloe began, "where are you from? Are your parents in the military? Most students' parents here are stationed at Otis but we have a few kids that live in Bourne." I smiled a little because for the first time I felt that things were going to be ok. Chloe seemed cool. She kept asking questions that made me feel like she wanted to get to know me.

"I'm from all over really. My mom is in the Air Force and has been stationed everywhere. I was born in Boston; my mom was on leave when she had me. I've lived in California, North Dakota, and Italy. I don't have any brothers or sisters and never knew my dad. We live up the street with my grandmother." I could see Chloe and Sebastian's eyes widen with excitement and sadness.

"You never knew your dad?" Chloe asked.

"No. I know he was in the Marines but that's all I know." I said. Chloe and Sebastian seemed to notice my sadness and frustration as they both tried to change the subject. Chloe put her arm around me and said, "Military life can be tough, Riley. Us military kids have to stick together, ya know? You can hang with us anytime."

"You lived in Italy?" exclaimed Sebastian. completely missing the sentimental stuff between Chloe and me. "That is so cool. Tell us about it."

"Italy was amazing. I lived there when I was eight years old during the summer. My mom and I lived on base and the camp I went to while my mom worked was within walking distance from our house. It had an awesome playground with a rock climbing wall, a pool and water park and a bunch of other fun things to do. The food was unbelievable too. We ended up leaving early because my mom got orders to go to a different base in the States for schooling. We had to…" I was half way into my story about living in Italy for a summer when the bell rang. I wish I had time to tell them about all the amazing food I had eaten and all the cool sights I had visited, but maybe next time.

"Riley, let's meet up after school. Sebastian and I can walk you home. I'd love to meet this grandmother of yours. Does she make cookies?" Chloe said with hope-filled eyes.

"She sure does and I wouldn't be surprised if she was making some chocolate chip cookies for me when I come home. I'll meet you outside the school after the bell." I left the table with a smile. As I looked back, I saw Sebastian giving Chloe a high five. I'm sure they were just as excited as I was. I closed my eyes for just a few seconds and let the anxiety of the day melt away. *So far, this was the best first day ever. I hope all my school days go this well.*

*****

Chloe and Sebastian decided to stay a little while after they walked me home. I'm pretty sure Sebastian is here to play ball and Chloe just wants the cookies I said my grandmother was making. Either way. It felt good to have some friends.

"Nice shot, Riley!" Sebastian shouted as my ball made another swish through the net. "You should really try out for the basketball team!" I found that the girls' basketball team could really use a shooting guard this season. They had one last year but I heard she is leaving with her family. I put up another basket and his face was shocked as the ball went into the hoop again. It made me blush a little.

"Thanks, Sebastian. I have thought about it. I used to play at my old school." *I was one of the best basketball players there.* "I really need to make sure I keep my grades up. I can already tell I'm behind in math." I was having trouble in math. I also really didn't want to get into the fact that my mother and I were having an argument over moving here and me having to give up my basketball dreams at my other school.

Chloe grabbed the ball from me and made her way toward the basket. She jumped a few feet from the net and her legs got caught underneath her. She fell back on her butt and laughed. "One of these days I'll make that shot!" She cried out in laughter and frustration. "I can't wait until I grow and actually be able to dunk the ball!"

Sebastian helped her up. "Riley, maybe you can help Chloe with her game and she can help you with your math?"

"Great idea! Let's sit down tomorrow in study hall and go over what you need help with, Riley." Chloe said and pushed Sebastian, playfully. "I may need help, but I can still kick your butt!" They both started laughing, which made me feel happy. These two were such good friends. *I hope that I can have this type of friendship with them too.*

"Sounds good to me… now let's work on your jump shot. Maybe this year we both can try out and rule the school with our skills." I laughed at my own attempt to be tough and grabbed the ball to make a shot.

SWISH! Chloe tried to block my shot but failed.

"Man, you are good!" Sebastian exclaimed. His eyes lit up again as he watched the ball gracefully enter the basket and bounce back toward her.

"Riley?!" Grandma called from the porch. "Do you and your friends want some chocolate chip cookies?" The amazing smell had been killing all of us for the last half hour.

"YES PLEASE!" We all shouted. I put down the basketball and we all ran up to the porch.

"You are awesome, Grandma!" I exclaimed. As much as I hated to admit it sometimes, I lucked out living here with my mom and grandma. She was so sweet and caring and had a funny personality. She didn't look like a grandma. Her hair was dark black and very straight. She had pale skin, soft complexion and I couldn't see many wrinkles. I looked over and saw Sebastian inhaling cookies as fast as he could. I wasn't surprised.

"Hey there, save some for me!" I smiled and reached for the milk and started to pour some for everyone.

"Riley, are you going to introduce me to your friends?" My grandmother asked. Her face was all smiles as she watched Sebastian inhale her famous cookies.

"Sorry, Grandma. This is Chloe Reagan and Sebastian Cook. They're both in my grade and I have some classes with them."

"Chloe and Sebastian, this is my grandma, Grandma Brown." Both of my new friends stood up and shook her hand. Chloe reached in for a hug.

"Wow! I am impressed, Riley. They both have good manners!" Grandma exclaimed. "It's nice to meet you both. I hope to see you around here. I'll make sure to keep some cookies in stock for this lad." And with a wink in Sebastian's direction she put more cookies on the plate and left the front porch.

I could hear the phone ringing just inside the front door. "I'll get it Grandma." I rolled my eyes a little to myself because I knew it was probably my mom calling to ask me how my day was. I didn't want to tell her how great it was because I was still a little mad about moving here to begin with.

"Hello?" I asked as I put the phone up to my ear.

"Hey, Riley, it's mom." I could hear planes in the background. "I don't have long but wanted to check in on you." She sounded tired.

"I'm doing good." I tried to sound a little upset that she wasn't here having cookies with me and meeting my friends. "School was ok. I made two new friends, Chloe, and Sebastian. They're over right now hanging out with me."

Mom let out a huge sigh. "That's great, Riley. I am so happy for you!" I could hear the relief in her voice. Suddenly, I heard some commotion in the background and lots of yelling.

"Hey, Riley- I have to go! I'm sorry. Things are not going well today and well... I'll see you tonight. I love you."

I sighed and thought, *yeah right, she's sorry she must go. She really loves her job more.* "Alright, Mom. See you later. I love you too. Bye." I hung up the phone, disappointed.

I wanted to cry. I was having such a good day and wanted to share everything with her. Even though she was my mom, we were best friends. Lately, I was so upset with her about moving again that it made me not want to talk about things. The argument before the move was very heated and I knew I had crossed the line with being disrespectful. I sat in the living room for a moment thinking back on the argument that happened six months earlier…

It was a beautiful day. The sun was shining and not a cloud in the sky. I had just come home from basketball practice. The season was over, but the girls still got together once a week to shoot some hoops and get tips from the coach. We were looking good for next year. Coach had pulled me aside and told me to keep up the hard work over the summer. I was the leading scorer and coach wanted ME to start next school year. I would be the only 8th grader on the varsity team. As I put my gym bag on the stairs, mom was sitting at the table with paperwork in her hand. The look on her face was one of a person getting coffee for the first time in the morning. Pure JOY.

"Hey mom! I can't wait to tell you the good news!" I exclaimed.

"I guess that makes two of us, Riley. I have some good news as well. Come and sit down and we'll talk about it." She sounded so happy.

"Coach said that I'll be starting on next year's team! He said that I if I keep playing the way I am that I have a good chance of getting a scholarship to a Division One school." I was grinning from ear to ear. I don't think anything could ruin my day right now.

Mom's face dropped. Clearly not the reaction I was looking for.

"Mom, what's wrong?" I thought she said she had good news to tell me. Can it be that she really isn't happy about me starting next year?

"We're moving, Riley. I got orders today." She didn't sound happy. I'm sure it was because she knew this was going to devastate me after the news I just gave her.

"WHAT?!?! WAIT…I thought we didn't have to move for another two and a half to three years? I thought the plan was that you were going to extend your stay here so I could at least start high school here?" My voice cracked as I yelled at my mom. Screw being respectful. I was so angry.

"Riley, calm down." My mom's voice was stern yet gentle. "I know this is not the plan but I have orders and there is nothing we can do. I was offered a job at Otis Air Force Base on Cape Cod and I think it will be a great place…"

I cut my mom off mid-sentence. "I DON'T WANT TO MOVE! YOU ONLY THINK ABOUT YOURSELF AND THE STUPID AIR FORCE!" I couldn't believe I was yelling at my mom. I took a deep breath and started again a little more calmly, "I don't want to move, Mom. I want to stay here. I'm tired of moving because of your job. I don't want to leave my friends and my teammates. Coach says I really have a chance at getting a scholarship if I play with him. Basketball is my life. PLEASE don't do this." I was

sobbing now, tears rolling down my face.

"Riley, please try to understand. I thought you…" I

didn't even let her finish her sentence.

"But Mom, what about my young group at church?

What am I supposed to do, just up and leave them while

we're in the middle of planning a mission trip for this

summer? Are you saying I won't be able to go? This was

supposed to be my best summer ever!" I cried even harder.

"I am sorry, Riley. I really am. This is a great

opportunity for us. I promise, this will be our last move. On

the upside, we'll be close to family and you'll love living

with your grandmother. She misses you so much. But no

matter how much you fight me, we leave at the end of the

school year and there is no changing that. I know that your

coach and team mean so much to you. I'm sorry but we

have no choice. We'll live with your grandmother for a

little while until I can find a house for us." My mom looked defeated.

I stormed out of the room, ran up the stairs to my bedroom, and slammed the door. I didn't want to hear another word.

"RILEY! COME DOWN HERE NOW!" My mom yelled from the bottom of the stairs.

I ignored it and turned my radio up loud. Who cares what happens to me. Let her ground me. She can't give me any worse punishment than she already has.

I didn't go out of my room the rest of the night as dinner didn't matter to me and there was no way I could see my mom right now. I was out of line for my outburst but was not ready to apologize for anything yet. When I woke up the next day and went downstairs, there was a note waiting for me.

Cereal is for breakfast and is on the table. Work called me in early, so I had to go in. I know you're angry and I'm sorry for that. I love you and want what is best for us. You will love the Cape, you really will. Have a good day at school, honey! Love, Mom.

I crinkled the note up, let out a huge sigh of frustration and went to get ready for school. I'll apologize when she comes home tonight, even though my heart wasn't fully in it right now. I was very disrespectful and there is no way mom deserved to be yelled at.

*****

"RILEY?" I could hear Sebastian and Chloe calling my name from the other room.

"Coming!" I put the house phone back in its cradle and grabbed my milk and cookies.

"You guys ready to play some more ball?" I said with excitement.

"Sure am!" Sebastian announced with some friendly competition in his voice.

Chloe didn't seem as enthused. She shuffled her feet and headed toward the street almost in a daze. "I think I'm going to head home. It's been fun. My parents are taking me out to dinner tonight and I want to make sure I'm ready." She explained. "See you both tomorrow in school."

"Sounds good, Chloe." I was already running down the front porch, racing toward the basketball. I waved toward Sasha as she grabbed her blue and pink North Face backpack and walked down the driveway. I thought I caught a hint of Chloe being upset as she left but quickly blew it off. *I'll make sure to ask her about it in school tomorrow.*

"How about a little one on one, Sebastian? Loser buys hot lunch tomorrow?" I asked.

"You're on, Riley. Better bring you're A-game!" he said with excitement and a little hesitation in his voice.

"Always do!" I shouted as he checked me the ball and then went up for a three-point shot.

SWISH! *This kid has no shot in beating me.* And with that, Sebastian and I played a little one on one until I came out victorious.

Chapter Three

Mom hadn't come home yet. I figure it had to do with all the yelling I heard in the background when she called earlier. I was going to use that to my full advantage. I figured we were already on the outs so why not break another rule and try to see what my mother and grandmother had to hide in the "forbidden attic." Since moving here a few weeks ago, I had free rein of the house. My mom was always at work as her new job was very demanding, and Grandma took care of me most of the time when she was not napping, baking, biking, walking or cooking. She was getting old and needed her rest but loved to stay active both physically and socially. I tried venturing up to the attic on my last visit but I never could find just the right time. I kept getting caught each time I tried to go up there. This was the perfect time, Mom was at work and Grandma would soon be asleep in her room, which was on the back side of the house.

"Grandma, I'm heading to bed!" I yelled from the top of the stairs.

"Ok. Good night, Riley!" She yelled back. "I'm heading to bed soon too!"

I knew she would be fast asleep within a minute from hitting her pillow. I climbed into bed and waited for ten minutes, looking at my clock watching the digital numbers climb higher and higher. "20:23, 20:24… 20:32, 20:34…" My clock seemed to move slower and slower. I kept it in military time since that's all my mom ever used. I didn't want to mess it up by getting the time wrong, so I used it too.

Once ten minutes was up, I tiptoed quietly upstairs to the attic where my grandmother kept all my mother's old things. I never understood why she kept so much of my mother's stuff, since she hadn't lived there in over a decade. Both my mother and grandmother told me when we arrived that the attic was off limits, but at this point I didn't care. My curiosity was getting the best of me. As much as I didn't care if I got in trouble, I kind of did care. Everything is so dusty up here, I thought as I made my way through the old boxes and furniture. There was a brown, old rocking horse placed over to the side. I think I remember seeing pictures of myself on this as a kid in one of the albums in grandma's living room. It was ratty by now and covered in a thick layer of dust. Why would someone keep this old thing?

The floor creaked very loudly as I walked across the room and I froze like a statue. I didn't want to wake grandma. I still had a few hours before my mom came home so I needed to be quick and quiet. I know she wouldn't want to scold me again for being in the one place that she forbade me from going, especially since we were already not in a good place after our fight. Her last words to me were, "Riley, if I catch you trying to go into the attic one more time, I am going to tan your hide!" I smiled a little because my mom had never spanked me in my whole life and I don't think she ever would. She would ground me though, and that would mean that I wouldn't be able to hang with my new friends, this weekend. I really didn't want to miss that.

I slowly started moving again and tried to make my footsteps lighter this time. I looked around the room; furniture was all stacked up and there were a ton of dusty old boxes. As I moved toward the back of the room, I saw a

box tucked away in the corner under the window. I picked
it up and brushed off the dust. "AAAHHHHCHOOO!!!" I
held my hand up to my face as I felt another sneeze come
on. I quietly silenced this one and kept my face covered.
The mildew odor was almost too much to bear. Why keep
all this junk upstairs if it's just going to sit up here and rot?
I thought to myself. I opened the lid of the box and found it
full of old photographs. They were black and white and
some had mildew on them, but I could make out the faces
of mom, grandpa and grandma, and a handsome looking
man in uniform. They all looked so happy. In the picture, I
saw what looked like my grandmother's house but it was
newer. The yard looked so pretty with huge rose bushes
surrounding the front step, a horse and paddock in the
background off to the side of house. This was definitely a
different time period. There were pictures of our town and
my mom and this man having fun. I decided to take the box
to my room and finish going through it down there. I had

less change of getting caught and getting in trouble. Pretty sure that I finally found what my mother did not want me to find.

As I opened my door to my room, I heard my mom's car pull into the driveway. I quickly tucked the box underneath my bed, turned off my light and jumped into bed. *I will go through the box tomorrow,* I thought to myself. With the box secretly tucked under my bed, I closed my eyes. I could hear my mom's radio playing Carrie Underwood's "Jesus take the wheel…" *At least we have the same taste in music*, I thought as I drifted to sleep.

******

I woke up early the next morning with an excitement that I hadn't had in a long time. I quickly went to the bathroom, took a shower, and got myself ready for the day, rushing back to get dressed in my room, I locked the door, pushed everything from underneath my bed and found the dusty old box. Opening it up, I found a letter on top that was unopened and looked old. It had my mother's name on it. *What the heck*, I thought, *might as well open it up since I've already gone this far.* As I broke the seal of the letter, my heart began to beat out of my chest. *Who was this letter from? Did my mother even know it existed and if so, why hadn't she opened it yet?* I wondered aloud in my own head. The paper unglued easily and I slide the paper out of the envelope and opened it.

My Dearest Sarah,

If you are reading this, I am gone. My platoon Sergeant told us that it was a good idea to write letters just in case something happened. I knew you would never take this so I gave it to your mother. Please don't be mad at her. She only did what I asked and kept this in case something happened. I cannot begin to tell you how much I love you. You mean the world to me and always have had my heart from the first day I met you. I'm sorry that I'm not there for you now. I just want you to know that I cannot wait to be a father and to watch you be a mother. I keep telling the other guys in my unit how my tough Air Force wife is going to be a mom and they are very happy for us. You're going to be a great mother. As I write this I think about the day we met back when we were 14 and 15 years old. I'll never forget you turning me down when I asked you to go on a date. It made me love you even more. You have always been a very driven woman and I love you for that. I pray that through the sadness of me being gone, you never lose that drive. I am so thankful that you opened your heart to me and let me love you and that you loved me back. I pray our little girl or boy knows that I love him/her very much. Please make sure they do.

I love you and always will,

Yours forever, Jeremiah

I sat on my bed, my eyes full of endless tears. These were my father's words. He never knew me but he loved me and wanted me. This was something that I needed to know. I had always felt so rejected not knowing my father or knowing if he ever loved me or held me. He was never talked about and now I wanted to know why. I was upset and confused, but happy to know that he loved me. I put the letter in my backpack and put the cover back on the box and slid it under my bed. I wanted to read the letter again and figured that school would be the best place to read it. I put some dirty clothes in front of it to ward off mom, grabbed my bag and headed downstairs to have breakfast. I must find out later what other secrets remained untold. *I should stop at the bathroom to clean myself up before Mom sees my tears.*

******

Pushing open the school doors, my heart was heavy and confused. *What else was up in that attic that could help me find out about my Dad?* I wasn't watching out where I was walking and bumped right into Mrs. Tanzy, my English teacher.

"Ooppps… sorry, Mrs. Tanzy!" I exclaimed. "I was in dream land."

"It's ok, Riley. I was preoccupied myself." Mrs. Tanzy replied. Her voice was kind but it had a hint of aggravation in it. She picked up the paperwork that she had dropped and I reached to help her.

"I've got it, Riley." She snapped in a little bit of a harsh tone. I quickly withdrew and gave her a quizzical look as I handed her back the papers she had dropped.

"Sorry, Mrs. Tanzy, I was only trying to help." I said in a smaller voice.

"It's ok. Now run along and get to class. I don't want you to be late." She exclaimed and turned and walked away in a hurry.

"Ok." I replied. *What is her problem?* Just then I realized the paperwork that I handed back to her had the words "divorce," "adultery" and a bunch of pictures of a man kissing a woman. It all looked like legal paperwork that I would see occasionally when my Mom was getting reassigned. *Poor Mrs. Tanzy, she's such a nice lady*, I thought. In my mind, I began to jump to so many conclusions. *I sure hope Mr. Tanzy isn't cheating.*

DING! *Oh no, that's the bell,* I thought. I picked up the pace and rushed to math class down the hall. Chloe was the first person I saw when I entered the classroom. I mouthed the words, "I need to talk to you after class. Meet me in the bathroom."

"Ok." She mouthed back, and gave me a weird look.

"Class, take your seat and open to page twelve. We will be going over multiplying rational numbers." Mr.

Dogherty announced. He looked over his shoulder and gave me the "evil eye" as I was still standing in the doorway and not in my seat.

"Care to join the rest of the class, Miss Tanner?" he asked with a hint of sarcasm in his voice.

"Sorry, Mr. Dogherty." I was a little embarrassed. My face turned bright red, but I had too much on my mind to really care about what the rest of the class thought of me. *I'll talk to Chloe about Mrs. Tanzy after class and maybe we can figure a way out to help her.* I opened my book to page twelve and began to copy what Mr. Dogherty was writing on the board.

Chapter Four

Coming home, I walked upstairs, put my bag away in my room, and changed my clothes to meet up with Chloe. She said she would come over since we couldn't talk in school. I want to continue my investigation into my mother's past but decided to wait until another time. It had been a week since I was in the attic and found some of my mother's old things and the letter from my father. I kept finding out more about my mother, grandmother, and father than I ever knew before. An old basketball, a bunch of men's clothes, a few marine uniforms, and lots of paperwork were just a few of the things that were hidden in this room. After I moved the desk, I found the initials J.T. and S.B. scribbled into the wooden beam.

As I opened the door, I almost peed myself when I saw my mother sitting on my bed. *Wow! I hadn't even noticed that her car was parked in the street when the bus dropped me off.* The brown box that I had taken from the attic was on the bed; photographs were everywhere.

Oh crap, I was caught! I guess the saying that moms know EVERTHING is true.

Before I could blurt anything, my mom spoke up first.

"Hi, Riley. I was coming to make peace. The tension between us has been getting too much for me so I got out of work early today and thought you would be home sooner. I saw some clothes near the end of the bed and found this box when I went to pick them up. I understand that this move has been hard on you and wanted to take you out for a movie and then dinner. I just never realized how bad our relationship really was. You're going through my stuff in the attic, yelling at me, disobeying me, and giving me attitude at every turn. I am…" She stopped midsentence. Her eyes welled up with tears and I noticed the deep black circles under her eyes.

"I'm sorry, mom!" I spit it out before she could go on any further. Tears were running down my face. I could tell by her face that she was upset and I didn't like knowing that I had made her feel sad. *I've been such a pain in the butt to her lately.* She looked so tired and upset.

Mom took a deep breath and I saw tears streaming down her face. "Thank you for saying that. I forgive you. It's time you and I had a talk." She held the box in her hands and looked at it with such sadness.

"This box is filled with so many memories, both happy and painful," mom began. "I was about your age when I met your father, Jeremiah Tanner. We met at the bus stop. We both had gotten detention and had to take the late bus home. Your father was tall and very handsome. It was raining and he gave me his umbrella to use. I was already drenched and didn't really need it but I took it anyways…"

Eighteen years earlier…

"Hey, you're Sarah, right?" Jeremiah called out, knowing full well who she was.

"Yea, that's me." Sarah replied. *She was soaked from head to toe. The weather hadn't called for rain but there they were, both wet from the torrential downpours.*

"I'm Jeremiah. Want my umbrella? You might be able to keep yourself from getting any wetter." He said with a voice so sweet Sarah could have kissed him.

"Thanks, want to share it? The bus should be here soon and I don't have cooties." Sarah laughed. She had never flirted with a guy before but for some reason Jeremiah had this way about him that made her want to.

"I'll have to bend down since I'm a little taller than you but sounds good." Jeremiah seemed clueless to the flirting and made his way closer to Sarah. He could see the bus in the distance so he knew it wouldn't be too long that they would be standing together. His heart was pounding out of his chest but he didn't want to let Sarah know that. She was the prettiest girl in school. He wondered what she

got detention for. Standing under the umbrella unable to speak, the two of them seemed content not to say anything at all. As the bus pulled up, Sarah broke the silence and stepped out from underneath the umbrella first.

"Thank you, Jeremiah." she whispered and stepped onto the bus.

He just stood there and watched her for a minute before following her. I'll marry that girl someday, *he thought to himself.*

Present day…

I looked at my mom, who seemed off in the distance. She was now holding an old picture of a young girl and boy holding an umbrella together. It almost looked like a selfie but poorly taken. She had tears rolling down her eyes and just sat there staring at it.

"Mom?" I said quietly. "You ok?" I didn't know what to really say. I began to see why she didn't want me going through her stuff.

"Riley, can we talk some other time?" I could see that she was upset so I didn't push for an explanation. She picked up the box and said, "I'm going to take this back to the attic. We can go through them later."

"Ok, Mom." I didn't hide my disappointment. *If they're going back to the attic we'll NEVER talk about them* is what ran through my head, but I held my tongue.

Mom left the room. I sat on my bed and thought about the letter that I didn't put back in the box. *Should I give it to her?* After a few minutes of debating it in my head, I decided to hold onto it for now and ask Chloe what I should do. I grabbed my basketball and headed outside to meet up with Chloe. First a quick stop in the bathroom. If mom didn't want to talk, then I would talk to my friends.

As Chloe had said, *us military kids must stick together, right?*

Chapter Five

I could see Chloe riding her bike up my driveway through the bathroom window. After parking her bike in the driveway, she walked up to front door. I left the bathroom and went down the stairs just in time to hear my grandma answering the door.

"Hi, Darling! How was school today?" my grandmother asked Chloe in a very endearing voice. I watched as Grandma's face showed complete joy when Chloe walked into the room. She looked at Chloe who was dressed in blue leggings, a bright hot pink top that went almost to her knees and high black boots and smiled brightly.

"It was good. It was busy and I have a lot of homework tonight. Riley and I are going to play some basketball at the courts and then do homework." Chloe explained.

"Is she home yet?" Chloe asked, her eyes wandering in the direction of the kitchen as the smell wafted out of the small area into the breezeway.

"She's upstairs changing. I'll call her down. Why don't you sit at the breakfast nook and have some cookies I just took out of the oven? I can see you glancing in that direction, young lady." Grandma winked at Chloe and headed toward the stairs.

Chloe smiled to herself and exclaimed, "Grandma Brown, don't mind if I do. You make the best cookies ever. I hate to admit it but you make them better than my grandmother did."

"Well, then, my dear, you'll just have to keep coming back and one day maybe I'll show you how to make them yourself." Grandma Brown said with a grin and smiled.

"Riley… Chloe is…" Grandma cried out.

"Right here, Grandma."

"Ah, how long have you been standing there, young lady? I didn't even hear you come down the stairs! Wow! I must be getting hard of hearing at my young age!" She winked at the two of us, which made us giggle. You two have fun. I'll see you for dinner." And with that she left us alone.

"Hey Chloe!" I said. Chloe turned around to see me standing with her basketball at the front door.

"Hey, Riley. Want a chocolate chip cookie?" Chloe asked with a sheepish grin.

"No, thanks. I'm good for now." I said. "I already snagged a few earlier when Grandma wasn't looking." Chloe normally would have laughed at that statement and would have commented on how clever I was for sneaking cookies. She just shrugged her shoulders instead. *What is up with her?*

"Ok. Well, do you want to get out of here and play some ball at the park? I could use some distraction." Sasha had just popped the cookie in her mouth and looked like she wanted to cry.

"Yea, sounds good. Let me just tell my grandma that I'm leaving now." I said and opened the door to find grandma.

A few minutes later, I was ready to go. Grandma just told me to make sure I was home in time for dinner. Chloe was already waiting by the end of the driveway. *I guess she really does want to get out of here. Was it something I did?* I wondered.

"Is everything ok, Chloe? You look upset. Did I do something?" I felt hesitant to ask because I hated when people cried, it always made me want to cry.

"No, you didn't do anything wrong. My parents are always fighting and I just can't take it anymore." She blurted out.

"I'm so sorry." My face clearly was showing sadness and hopped it didn't make her uncomfortable. Dribbling while walking stopped so there was less noise while she talked as I wanted her to know she had my full attention.

"It's ok. Thanks for saying that. My grandmother died not too long ago and my mother has been so different. She stays in her room a lot and barely gets things ready anymore for my brother and me." She went on to explain. "I try to talk to her but she just gets mad at me. My dad said to just try and stay out of her way and that she is just sad about grandma. I guess I just don't understand why she has to be mean to all of us." Sasha sat down as we got to the benches by the park basketball courts and put her head down and cried. "I just want my mom to go back to normal. She and my dad used to be so happy. We used to do so many fun things together as a family and now we don't."

I looked around and hoped no one was watching. There wasn't anyone at the court this time of day. Most kids went to the afterschool program on base but Chloe and I didn't, so it was just us at the courts. I just hoped Sebastian didn't show up. Neither Chloe or mye have been hanging out with him much anymore. He started hanging out with this girl named Charlotte Will who was a year ahead of us and was kind of off the grid. The gossip around school is that they were dating and spending all their time together at her house. Either way, I don't think Chloe would be comfortable with him showing up right now in the middle of her meltdown.

"I'm not sure what to say. I think that your mom is having a hard time with your grandmother dying. Maybe if you tried just writing her a note and tell her how you feel that might help." I reached into my gym bag, grabbed some tissues, and handed them to her. Here I am giving her advice when my mom and I were on the outs. *I feel like such a hypocrite.*

"Thanks." Chloe said. "Sorry I lost it just then," she said with an embarrassing look on her face as she wiped her face and blew her nose.

"No problem, it happens." I was still getting to know Chloe so I didn't want to over step my bounds too much in the advice department, but decided to give it a shot.

"So, my Grandma tells me that when I'm stressed out not to worry. She says that praying and remembering that God has a plan always helps her when she feels overwhelmed. I can't remember the Bible verse she uses, or if you even know what the Bible is but it helps me when she reads it." As I finished my sentence, I looked over to see Chloe smiling.

"My grandmother used to read me the same verse." Chloe explained. "It's from Jeremiah 29; It pretty much says that God has a plan for us."

She put her arm around me and said, "Thanks, girl! I needed to hear that." And with that, she grabbed the basketball and started to dribble it. "Your grandmother reminds me so much of my own. She is amazing, Riley!"

"I agree and she sure likes you, Chloe!" I exclaimed. "I don't think she has ever said to any of my friends that she would give them the secret ingredients to her cookie recipe!"

My head was in the clouds. I thought, maybe Chloe was a friend that I could talk about my faith with. *How great would that be and who would have thought? I wonder if she has ever gone to a youth group?* I think that will be a conversation for a different time. And she loves my grandma. Life is looking up for me in this town. Maybe I can cut my mom a little slack on this moving thing.

"Enough about me and my family drama, Riley. What did you want to talk to me about so bad in class today?" Chloe looked at me curiously as she threw me the ball.

Again, here I go with taking a leap of faith and just speaking my mind. I didn't want to upset her as she just broke down crying about her parents and the possibility of them getting a divorce. "It's not the greatest news. I know you're upset about your parents so maybe we can talk about it another time." I tried to deflect the conversation.

"Riley, come on. I'll be fine. Thanks for watching out, but I'm not that fragile." Chloe said.

"Ok. Well, I ran into Mrs. Tanzy today in the hall and she was upset. I knocked over papers she was carrying and tried to help her pick them up, but she didn't want me to and snapped at me." Chloe had a concerned look on her face.

"Mrs. Tanzy isn't one to snap, especially when it's an accident and the student offers to help. I wonder what's up?"

"Well, here's the thing, she had legal paperwork in her hand and there were pictures of a man and a woman kissing. I don't know who they were but I can only assume that it is her husband." I explained. "Do you know what Mr. Tanzy looks like?" I asked.

"Yes, I remember what he looks like. He is soooo cute." Chloe's eyes rolled and she got that dreamy look on her face. "He's a firefighter in town. He has light hair and is tall. He came in around Halloween last year to do a demonstration with his entire crew for the school."

"Does she keep pictures on her desk of her husband?" I asked. I honestly didn't remember but thought Chloe would since she had Mrs. Tanzy the previous year.

"She does. We should check it out. Do you think you'll remember what the guy looked like in the picture?" Chloe asked.

"I sure will. He was really cute for an older guy and now that you mention it I think there was a fire truck in the background of the picture."

"Well, let's try and get to class a little early and figure this out. Maybe we can find a way to help her. If Mr. Tanzy is cheating and they're getting a divorce she'll need some support. I get that we'ee kids but we can still help a little, right?" Chloe said with a good amount of determination in her voice.

"Right!" I said. "I'll get to school early tomorrow. I'm sure Grandma won't mind bringing me a little early."

"Hey guys!" said a male voice. We both turned around to see Sebastian and his new "girlfriend" heading over to us. "I didn't realize you'd be here." Sebastian said with a shy and hesitant grin. "This is my friend, Charlotte." He gave us a look that told us to go easy.

Oh man… this doesn't look like it's going to be fun. I didn't realize he was going to bring his possible girlfriend, I thought to myself as my face turned bright red. *And why am I all flustered anyways…* it's just Sebastian.

Chloe nudged me forward. I gave her the evil eye that I hoped neither Charlotte nor Sebastian had caught. "Hi, Charlotte. I'm Riley and this is Chloe. Nice to meet you!" I said in my friendliest voice. I really was trying to be genuine, as I stuck my hand out to shake her hand which she accepted.

"It's nice to finally meet you, Riley. I've heard so much about you." And with that she winked at Sebastian and grabbed the ball from him to take a shot.

"Oh, really. Well we haven't heard anything about you, Charlotte!" I exclaimed and went and got her rebound.

Chloe walked over and gave Sebastian a playful punch in the arm as Charlotte and I were shooting some hoops under the net. "Where have you been the last week or so, kid? You've like dropped off the face of the planet and never return our calls anymore. What's the deal? We miss hanging with you."

Sebastian looked over at Charlotte and spoke quietly. "I've been hanging with Charlotte. I don't want to talk about it right now if that is ok with you." Chloe gave him a weird look and grabbed the ball that was on the ground.

"Charlotte, do you like to play ball?" Sasha asked with a chuckle in her voice.

"Not really, but this guy does," pointing at Sebastian, "so I'll join in. What are we playing?" she said completely oblivious to the tension that was happening between friends.

"How about a little two on two? Riley and me against Sebastian and you?" Chloe said with a grin. "Winner gets ice cream when the truck comes by."

"Go easy on me girls," Charlotte cried out. "It's just a friendly game here. If you're anything like Sebastian, this game will be pretty intense."

Sebastian nervously laughed and threw the ball to me. "Good luck, Riley," he said.

"Ha, you're going to need it, Sebastian." I said. I took the first shot and made three points for Chloe and me.

The game was a long one and I felt completely embarrassed. Charlotte was apparently a very good ball player and Chloe and I found that out a little too late. Since neither one of us brought money for ice cream we told them we would owe them one, gathered up our stuff and walked home. I left the court confused. Sebastian was clearly flirting with me during the game but hanging out with another girl all the time. I just didn't get it. Maybe I will talk to him tomorrow about it. I just want to figure out what is going on here and I don't want to lose a friend. *I was a little jealous that he was spending so much time with Charlotte.* Chloe kept walking past my house, toward hers and I went inside mine. Grandma and mom were waiting for me when I got home for dinner.

Chapter Six

It had already been a few weeks into the new school year and we were all settling into a new routine with work and school. Mom left for work before I got up and got home long after I was in bed. She always left notes for me in the morning and packed my lunch so I didn't have to buy at school. Grandma was home with me in the afternoon and had no problem if my friends came over. Chloe was a regular at my house, especially since things were getting bad at her home with her parents. No more had been talked about with mom about the attic and I knew to leave well enough alone.

Grandma's voice broke into my thoughts. "Riley, I'm heading to Bible study with the ladies. I won't be home until around 8:30." Grandma didn't like using military time. It kind of made me laugh since Mom and I used it all the time.

I got up from my chair and gave her a big hug. "Ok, Grandma. I love you. Have fun with your ladies."

Bible study was where my grandmother and a few of her lady friends from church got together over tea and dessert and read from the Bible. She explained to me that sometimes they would read from a book that helped them study the Bible more and everyone shared their thoughts about it. She said that they sometimes just talked and prayed. Every time she came home, she always looked a little fresher than before she left. I assumed it was kind of like youth group but just with other people. Just thinking about this made me miss my friends from Langley Air Force Base. They sent me tons of pictures from their mission trip over the summer and I saw the Facebook page that was created. They helped build a family a new house and had so much fun at the church services and meetings. *I'm so jealous and I wish I had been there.*

Grandma grabbed her keys and blew me a kiss as she walked out the door. As I locked the door behind her, all I could think of now was that I was going to be home by myself which meant I could do a little more snooping in the attic. I ran upstairs and opened the attic door. It still had that same gross musty smell to it but it was starting to grow on me. I walked past the beam that was initialed "JT + SB" and traced my fingers along the lettering. I sat down on the old wooden rocking chair in the corner of the room. It made the floor creek a little but it didn't matter to me since no one was home. I pulled out one of the books in the boxes in front of me. It was a maroon color and leather bound, it had my mother's initials engraved on the front, "S.R.B." It also had a little bit of mold because of the dampness in the attic, but the pages were legible. I turned to the first page and found my mother's name and date of birth. *What a great find!* I thought to myself. I sat back down in the rocking chair started to read the first entry.

Day One

I read somewhere once that it was helpful to keep a journal when a loved one was deployed or deathly sick, so they'll know what you went through. I decided to give it a shot, so here goes.

I just dropped Jeremiah off at Westover Air Force Base and said goodbye to him as he boarded the bus that would take them to the C-5's. I knew exactly where they were going and wanted to follow them just to catch another glimpse of him before he left on his tour. I hate that it had to be this way. I wanted to scream and yell and tell him to get off the plane but I didn't. My heart knows he's doing what he loves and that's serving his country. He's a Marine and he loves his job with all his heart, just as much as I love my job in the Air Force. My belly's jumping around and my maternity shirt is dancing a little. I can't help but smile in such a sad time. We're having a baby! We are not finding out the sex so we need to be prepared with a girl and boy name. Jeremiah refuses to figure out a boy's name as he knows the baby will be a girl. He has his heart stuck on Riley and I want Rose so I am not sure how we are going to figure out how to name her. And she could turn out to be a boy, so who knows.

WOW! I stopped for a second to think about what I just read. Did my mom just write that my dad had picked out my name? Man, I wish she would just tell me this herself. I hate sneaking behind her back and reading her journals and letters to find out what happened. I jumped out of my thoughts and continued reading.

We will get through this. It is only a six-month deployment but it is to Al Assad, Iraq. This region isn't the safest place but it isn't Fallujah so it could be worse. I can't write much more. I have to get home to my mom's house and get ready to head back to Texas. I have to report back for duty in a few days. Hopefully things will go as planned and in 3 months, our baby girl or boy will arrive and we'll settle in our new home on base. Three months after that, Jeremiah will join us, and we'll continue our journey on being a family. He was going to change career fields and become an officer. He finished his degree and is going to Officer Candidate School a few months after he returned from deployment. Jeremiah is a patriotic and loyal soul. He wanted to make sure his men made it home safe and while he didn't have to deploy with his unit, he chose to. I commended him for that but at the same time, it was a topic of some very heated discussions. In the end, I knew I could not ask him to give up something that I wouldn't if I was in his shoes. I am sure that is why we love each other so much. We both understand the call to serve. It is something that those who have the same calling can truly understand.

But trust me I wish this wasn't happening now. I wish he was coming to home for the birth of our baby and I was so frustrated that I was doing this pregnancy thing on my own. I wanted him here every step of the way. My mom would be with me a lot but she would eventually have to go back to her own life and her routine. Well, that is enough venting for now. I guess writing is helpful. Time to get on the road. I will write again. Love you always and forever, Jeremiah.

Your Sarah

I put the journal down and then realized my hands were shaking. I think I now understand why mom doesn't want to talk about this stuff. I wiped away my tears with my sleeve and put the journal back in the box. These memories were painful and I didn't live them. My mom loved my dad so much and it seems he loved her too. I wonder if she feels guilty about letting him go to war? As curious as I was, I couldn't read any more of my mom's journal, at least right now. I began to look through other boxes. I found a pair of roller skates that had crayon all over them and I remember a picture of myself in them so I was delighted to find a box that had some of my old stuff in it. I found my first report card, a picture that I had drawn for my mom and little box that held some gross looking little teeth. I always wondered what parents did with baby teeth that fell out and now I know. I went through about five boxes and then wrapped up my search for answers. Figuring that grandma would be home soon and I still needed to shower and do some reading before bed, I looked in the direction of the box where I laid the journal and whispered, I'll be back to read you. I made sure things were neat and headed back toward the door, brushing my parents' initials in the wooden beam. As I walked down the stairs, I gently turned off the light switch and closed the door. I figured I have a lifetime to figure out what happened to my dad and why it's so painful for my mom to talk about, and there is no rush in finding out. Sebastian had said that he has lived in this town all his life. Maybe his parents knew my mom and dad when they were younger and they could tell me what happened.

Little did I know that I didn't push the light-switch down hard enough and the light stayed on.

Chapter Seven

"Hey Sebastian," I called to him as he was walking down the hall.

He turned around and said "Hi, Riley. What's up?" His voice sounded a little hesitant but he had a smile on his face so I guess he was happy to see me.

Things the other day were awkward at the park with his new friend, Charlotte, and I wanted to make sure we all were still cool. The last thing I wanted was to lose a friend that I just had made.

"Are we ok?" I asked. I thought it was better to just cut to the chase.

"Yeah, we are. Was it me, or were things a little tense and awkward the other day at the courts? Sorry, if I caught you and Chloe off guard bringing Charlotte to play ball." Wow! *He didn't waste any time explaining things, so this was good.*

"It's ok, but are you ready to answer the million-dollar question that everyone wants to know?" I said it kind of playfully, not wanting to really know the answer and not sure why.

"Are Charlotte and I dating? Is THAT the million-dollar question?" The way he over- emphasized the words made my face turned bright with embarrassment.

Man, he caught me off guard. *WHY was I acting like a complete idiot*? I thought. I shifted my feet uncomfortably and looked up at him for a moment. "Yes, that's the question?" I said softly, trying to make as little eye contact as possible.

He moved closer and whispered in my ear, "No, we're not dating. I don't like her like that, Riley." I looked up at him. He was a few inches taller than me and my heart was pounding. Our eyes locked for a quick second. He leaned in toward me and I thought he was going to kiss me right there in the middle of the hallway. Right in the middle of kids walking in and out of classrooms, rushing to get to class on time. Right in front of our teachers and...*This can't happen.*

I pushed him away very playfully and started to laugh. "You are something else. You know how many rumors are going around here about you and Charlotte?" I completely hid the fact that I would have kissed him if he leaned in any further.

He stepped back playfully and put his arms up in the air. "What can I say? I can't help it if people talk. Our parents know each other, and they've been getting together a lot lately because they're moving. Both of our dads are in the same unit and are heading out over to Italy for a few years. She tags along with them. She likes video games and so do I so we always have fun hanging out." He seemed to push past the moment and acted like nothing had happened.

"Well, that's good to hear. Chloe and I miss hanging out with you. Come over anytime and bring Charlotte. She is your friend, so she'll be ours." I said quickly, hoping the bell would ring and give me an escape. *Am I falling for my new friend?* I thought. *Oh, Gosh I hope not.*

"Sounds good, Riley. Thank you for being you. See you at lunch. Later, kid" He winked and turned toward homeroom.

I stood there for a minute and let my heart feel what I just felt. *I like Sebastian.* My heart and my head were saying the same thing. I stared at him as he walked into homeroom, his back to me. Just as I was about to turn, he looked back and gave me a sheepish smile, winked, and disappeared behind the door.

Oh no... *He likes me too.* His look and boyish grin said it all... and his wink... my heart skipped a beat. I grabbed my science book out of my locker and ran to class. I had to get out of my head and fast. Science class would be a good way to do that.

*****

"Swish!" Man, I love that sound, I thought as the ball went into the net and bounced back to me. Tryouts were underway, and I was in the middle of showing off my three point skills. I wanted to try out for point guard but Sebastian and Chloe convinced me that shooting guard would probably be the best position for me. Neither Sebastian nor I mentioned our moment we had in the hallway the day before. Deciding to ignore it for now, was the best thing. I had basketball tryouts, math to catch up on, my relationship with my mom to make better, and a full boatload of issues to figure out. Being the new girl wasn't easy especially when there were a lot of girls pining over Sebastian. *A lot of other girls prettier than me.*

As I looked over and saw Coach Roberts on the side line, he was talking to some of the other kids and giving them pointers on how to play "around the world." I told him at the beginning that I knew how to play so he had me go first. He was a tall man with a balding head and a red face, which made it seem like he was mad; But I already was told by some of the players that he was a big teddy bear.

"Riley, you're up next!" Coach yelled. "Just stay calm and focus. You got this!" He was so encouraging but I still had the butterflies. *I wish my mom was here.*

Taking my place on the three-point line, my heart raced. *Get your head in the game, Riley. Don't screw this up over a boy!* I stepped up to the line, gripped the ball and stared at the basket allowing the ball the bounce twice as I shifted my feet. The coach's eyes seemed to be burning through me as I prepared myself for the next 2 minutes of shooting. The point of this exercise was to get as far as I could around the different spots around the basket. Missing shots meant starting over which would not be good. The clock was set for two minutes. The coach gave the signal to start the 10 second clock which would buzz when the timer went off and it was my queue to begin. I dribbled the ball again and looked over into the crowd.

"You can do this, Riley!" I heard the voice and saw the person but couldn't believe my eyes. *My mom had made my tryouts.* She gave me a small wave and thumbs up. That gave me the vote of confidence that I needed. The butterfly's cleared out of my stomach as I put my feet up to the line. *I'm ready.* The buzzer went off and a second later the ball was leaving my hands. SWISH!

The next two minutes seem to be the longest of my life. I had to start over once but then I made it all the way around the world and was going back when the timer went off.

"You set the bar high, Riley. Great job," Coach said as he gave me a high five. "Grab a drink of water and come back to the side-line to cheer on the other girls."

"Yes, Coach," I said with excitement in my voice. I glanced over to the side lines and could see my mom waving. She walked down the bleachers and handed me a bottle of water.

"You did a great job, Riley. I'm proud of you!" Mom said with a huge grin on her face.

"Thanks, Mom. I'm glad you made it... I can't talk long but I'll see you afterward for ice cream?"

"You got it, Riley!"

Making my way back to the court to cheer on the rest of the girls trying out, I thought how it was a nice surprise to see my mom at my basketball tryouts. Her work was demanding so this was a huge effort on her part to show me she cared. Looking back toward the bleachers, I saw that she was talking on her phone, eyebrows raised and looking wicked mad. *I guess this means we won't be going out for ice cream.* A huge rush of emotion came over me and my lip began to curl as I turned away. *Don't lose it, Riley.* Crying can wait until later. Maybe she wouldn't have to leave. I hesitantly looked back toward where she was sitting. She wasn't there. I looked over to the door and saw her waving at me. She mouthed the words, "So sorry!" and pushed the gym door open. My heart sank but neither one of us could change the situation. I looked back at the court and clapped for the girl who just finished her portion of around the world. *At least there's basketball, right?*

Chapter Eight

Friday was finally here, and I couldn't wait to find out if I had made the team. Coach said he would post the team roster on his door after lunch. I figured I could head down to his office before gym class since the girl's locker room was right down the hall.

The rest of tryouts went well, at least I think they did. There were a few other players that had made it further than I did in around the world. We ran lots of sprints and I was the fastest. Coach had us sub in for some of the girls in a full court game. He said it was a way of seeing if we could keep up with rest of the team and to see where we fit. I felt like I kept up with the rest of the girls. Some of the girls on the team were great players.

Tara Raven was the shooting guard on the team and I wanted her position. Coach said she was leaving in the middle of the season so her spot would be open. When I sat on the sidelines during the tryouts, I made sure to keep an eye on her and see what I could learn. She had great form and always made herself available for a pass or shot. She just seemed to know where the ball was going and made it there to make the play. She was talented. I almost felt bad wanting her spot so much. Either way, I just wanted to play on the team, regardless of my position.

The loud hallways brought me back to reality. Sometimes I wish that my teachers would release us a few minutes before the bell so I would miss the pushing and shoving in the halls. Everyone was always rushing to get to class and didn't care about who they bumped on the way. I already had my books knocked out of my hands so many times. English class was next, and I was trying to think of a way to get out of it. Sebastian and I were back to being normal friends but I couldn't help the feeling of wanting to avoid him. I knew I had a crush on him, but I didn't want to take it any further than just a crush. I blushed every time we talked and I just needed some time to get my red face under control. Maybe Chloe has some good advice about this. She's known Sebastian longer than I have. I walked into English fully expecting my face to turn red, but Sebastian's chair was empty. Come to think of it, I hadn't seen him all day. Normally, we see each other in the hall before Math but I must have been too preoccupied with basketball to even notice.

"Riley?" Mrs. Tanzy's voice entered my mind. I must have been day-dreaming during attendance.

"Yes, I'm here." I exclaimed.

"Wake up, class. Riley isn't the first person I have had to call on twice. When you hear your name, let me know you're here. Everyone, understand?" Mrs. Tanzy didn't sound happy. "After I mark you here, you can take out your journals and start writing your entry for today. Do not forget to leave them on your desk after class. I'll be looking at them over the weekend." Her voice was tense, and her scowl showed a different side of her that I wasn't used to. Her voice was usually soft and her teeth were always showing from smiling so much. Some of my classmates turned around and laughed but I ignored them.

I only have had her for two months, but man she has changed. Way grumpier now. I looked at Karin next to me and we both rolled our eyes. Pretty sure we were thinking the same thing. Grumpy Mrs. Tanzy! I took out my notebook and began to write out my thoughts for the day. I like this assignment. Each day, Mrs. Tanzy wanted us to write a paragraph about anything we wanted to. Here is what I wrote today,

> *"I'm super excited about finding out if I made the basketball team but very also very nervous. There were so many good players and I just want to play ball. One of my teachers is not happy these days and I wish I knew how to help. My mom and I are still on the outs, but she came to my tryout and that made me think that things will get better. I'm reading a Nancy Drew book and will probably finish it tonight. My mom makes me read for at least*

a half hour a day so I'm finishing it fast. I find out if

I made the team in less than an hour."

I wanted to add more to my entry but the teacher was already starting to talk about the project that we had coming up and I didn't want to miss it. I looked to the left and saw that Sebastian's chair was still empty. I guess he wasn't going to make it. Maybe Chloe knew where he was. We have lunch together next period. Mrs. Tanzy's assistant started to hand out the outline for our project. I asked for another one in case Sebastian didn't get make up work. I tried to pay attention the rest of the class but had a very hard time. There is always so much going on in my mind to think about. Why was Mrs. Tanzy so short tempered and grumpy? Where was Sebastian? Would I make the team?

RING! The bell sounded loud and clear. *Yes! Class is over for the day!* The words escaped my mouth before I could take them back. I am just happy Mrs. Tanzy or her assistant didn't hear me. I already felt like I was in hot water with her and didn't want anything getting in the way of me getting to coach's door after lunch. I packed up all my books, made my escape and found my way to Chloe's locker where we usually meet up.

When I got there, Chloe wasn't there. *She always gets here ahead of me.* I looked at my watch, 11:40. I'll wait for a few more minutes and then I'll head to the cafeteria. Maybe she would just meet me there. First, Sebastian wasn't in class and now Chloe wasn't at her locker. I tried not to think that something was the matter. The hall was beginning to empty so I decided to book it to lunch before it was over. As I walked into the lunch room, the smells almost made me throw up. It was fish sticks and I love those. They're my favorite hot lunch no matter what school I have been at. I hadn't had them from this school yet but I'm sure they are amazing. Today, my stomach couldn't even think of eating them. I took an apple and some crackers and sat down at our usual table by myself.

Where are my two friends? This is why I need a cell phone.
I couldn't help but worry. I tried to focus on something else
so I took out my Nancy Drew book and started reading. It
was hard to pay attention to the words because the cafeteria
was crazy loud. *I wish people would just be quiet. Did
everyone really need to bang their trays and yell to get
someone's attention?* I felt like I was beginning to come
down with something. My head hurt so bad and I started to
feel really cold. I felt my forehead and it didn't seem warm.
I tried to focus on my reading but no luck.

Just then, the bell rang, and lunch was over.
Looking over my food, I realized I barely ate any of it.
Nerves maybe? Heading down the hall toward coach's
office, now more worried about my friends than excited or
nervous about the list on his door. Maybe they both got
sick? Or maybe they would be waiting for me at coach's
door? I talked to Chloe last night and she didn't say
anything about being out of school today. Walking down

the hallway, my face felt hot and flushed and the room started to get dizzy. Seeing the water fountain, I took a huge drink, hoping that would help. My stomach began to feel awful and the next thing projectile vomit was everywhere. I leaned up against coach's door and looked around frantically for a bucket.

Mr. Connell, my science teacher, ran up to me and threw a bucket under my chin just as I hurled again. "Miss Riley, I take it you are not feeling well?" His voice almost sounded sarcastic.

"I feel horrible! I think…" my voice trailed off as I threw up again.

"Let's get you to the nurse's office." He said with a hint of disgust in is voice. He looked almost green as he held the bucket to my chin.

 As I walked past coach's door, I glanced just long enough to see my name on the list posted.

In a quiet voice, I exclaimed, "I made the team!"

"Congratulations, Riley!" He held the bucket closer as I started to hurl again. "Let's call your mother and see if we can get you home so you can actually play this year!"

I felt nothing about making the team. My previous excitement was overcome by the feeling like my head was going to explode. The floor looked so cold and looked so inviting. A few years ago I had the flu, and I laid down on the bathroom floor. The tiles were so cold and it helped my fever. My mom had to almost carry me into bed that day. I felt the same way today. Standing in the middle of the hallway, was Joey, watching, pointing, and laughing at me. His face was all smiles and he called out, "Hey pukey! Hahaha... Riley the puker! Hahaha!" *Man, I wish Chloe or Sebastian were here to help me!* He was the school bully and his father was high up in the chain of command so everyone thought he got away with a lot especially with most teachers.

Mr. Connell walked past him and glared at him and said "Joey, that's not nice. Stop it now and get to class!" At least one teacher stood up to him. I was in social studies last week and he started making fun of me because I was wearing a Celtics jersey. He started calling me a boy and was relentless about it. I talked to my teacher after class, and she just told me to ignore him and didn't stop him from making fun of me. I told my mom about it and she said she would do something if it continued.

Mr. Connell opened the nurse's office door and exclaimed, "Nurse, we have a puker!" He winked and then pointed me to a chair for me to sit in. I tried not to laugh because he was humorous. I guessed he was trying to make light of Joey making fun of me. He was a short man, and was going bald on top. If I had to guess, he was 35 years old. He did seem like he liked to go to the gym and could make you laugh; he was very smart.

"Another one?" Nurse Lisa exclaimed. She pulled back the curtain, "You," she said, "are the third one today!"

I stood up and almost shouted. "Chloe, Sebastian…" My friends were sitting with their heads over buckets. They both looked up and gave me half smiles. I was almost relieved.

"I take it you all know each other?!?" Nurse Lisa said with a smile. "Riley, I don't have another bed so why don't you stay seated in the chair. I'm going to have the nurse call someone to pick you up."

Sebastian spoke up, "Chloe and I have been in here since second period. The nurse can't get in touch with our parents. Is there any way your mom or grandma could take us home with you? Both are on our pick-up lists." He looked so green.

I thought for a minute and didn't think it would be a problem. He's so cute even when he's sick. *Darn it… there*

I go again. Get yourself together, Riley. "I'll ask the nurse to check with Grandma Brown. My mom probably won't pick up right away but Grandma will probably be here within ten minutes. I'm sure she will have no problem taking us all home. I'm just glad you both are somewhat ok. I was worried about the two of you." Chloe a smiled and put her head back in the bucket. I looked at Sebastian and he winked at me. I blushed. *He really has to stop winking at me.*

"Well, I'm glad that you don't have to worry anymore." Sebastian said. He was staring at me so intently, at least so I thought. "How was English class?" He said quietly.

"It wasn't too bad. Mrs. Tanzy was in a bad mood. I just wish I knew what was going on with her. Chloe and I are going to try and figure it out. Well, we were until we all got sick. I got you a copy of our project." I went to reach in my bag but then realized that it wasn't there.

At that moment, I couldn't remember where I put my backpack. The last time I remember having it was right before I was throwing up in the hallway. It must have dropped. I could feel the color draining from my face. I had a notebook in there that I didn't want anyone to see. It was my journal. I just prayed it didn't get into the wrong hands. Some kids in this school would love to cause trouble and share everything in that journal. Middle school could be a tough place if you were on the wrong side of bullying.

"You ok, Riley?" Chloe asked. Her head was out of the bucket and her face showed concern.

"I must have left my backpack in the hallway where I was throwing up!" I said nervously. I didn't care now that I was sick. All I wanted to do is look for my bag. I was about to say something else when Nurse Lisa came back into the room.

"Ok, all of you are going home with Riley's grandmother. She said she would make sure you get back to your parents. She should be here soon. I'll give each of you a bag to take with you in case you get sick. It looks like you all have a version of the flu. Rest up, stay hydrated and get some rest." Nurse Lisa spoke very kindly to all of us, handed each of us a vomit bag and left the room.

"What should I do?" I asked Chloe. "My journal is in my bag. I didn't mean to bring it to school but I was writing on the porch before school and just threw it in my bag."

"I would go…" She didn't even finish her sentence when there was a knock on the Nurses door.

A kid from my math class came through the door. I couldn't remember his name. "Hey, Riley, I have your bag. You dropped it earlier and someone gave it to me knowing we were in the same class.

"That's awesome, Riley!" Chloe exclaimed. "Jimmy, you are a life saver, right, Riley?"

"Yes, Jimmy! Thank you!" I sighed in relief. "You really did me a big favor. I owe you one."

I didn't even take the time to look in my bag for my journal. I started to feel sick again and put my head back in the bucket.

"Yea-ok, well I'm out of here. Get better, Riley!" He said as he walked out the door. His face looked as though he was going to throw up.

The door closed and I rested my head up on the side of the wall.

"Riley, come over here," Sebastian said. "You look horrible and I think I'm feeling the best out of all of us three." Chloe had rolled over and curled up on the little bed that was in the nurse's office. Sebastian was being very kind.

"Thanks, don't mind if I do." I walked over and slowly jumped onto the bed. "Move over, Sebastian." My heart was racing and I was praying that I wasn't showing it. I knew my face was already red but my stomach was making up for it by making it green. This was not romantic as we were all so sick but the gesture was very nice.

Sebastian scooted over and gave me enough room. Only our shoulders were touching. He grabbed my hand and held it tight. He looked at me and smiled. "I hope you feel better soon," he said.

"Me too!" I replied and with that I laid my head on his shoulder and fell asleep. Before I dozed off, I thought how nice this was and how much I wish I had checked my backpack for my journal.

Chapter Nine

I woke up to the sun shining in my face. The skylight in my room was like an annoying alarm clock except that you couldn't press snooze. I looked at my clock and decided to get up. It was almost 10:00. I grabbed my robe and headed downstairs. Grandma's car wasn't in the driveway so I knew she was at the early church service. She played the piano at the local church for two of the services. It was within walking distance so every Sunday I met her at church for the noon service. The last service was geared more toward the younger generation and the music team had their own pianist for the last service.

I felt like I had just woken up from a bad nightmare. Grandma picked all three of us up at school on Friday and we all spent the night vomiting. Chloe and Sebastian's parents came late Friday night to pick them up. Apparently, there was a squadron sendoff that most of the parents were required to attend and my grandmother said they could stay until it was over. I spent most of my day in bed and felt so much better this morning. *I can't wait to eat something.* When I reached the bottom of the stairs, I looked outside and saw mom sitting on the porch with her coffee. I felt so happy to see her and wanted so badly to tell her how much I've missed her.

"Hey mom! I'm surprised to see you home." I said to her.

"We had a good day yesterday and things are starting to look like they're settling down. It looks like I'll be home every Sunday from now on and an occasional Saturday as well." Mom explained.

"How are you feeling?" she asked. "Grandma said you were still out of it yesterday and she wasn't sure if you were going to make it to church today.

"I'm feeling a lot better and pretty hungry. Do you want some breakfast?" I asked my mom.

"Sure, what are you making?" Mom asked with a huge smile on her face.

"Good old-fashioned veggie omelets!" I exclaimed.

"When did you learn to cook eggs?"

"Grandma taught me. She's teaching me to cook and bake

all kinds of things including her famous cookies." I beamed with pride.

"Wow. I guess I've missed a lot these last few weeks." Mom said with a hint of sadness in her voice.

"Don't worry. Things will slow down. At least you have Sundays off now, right?" I said trying to cheer her up.

"You're right. Let me help you. I learned that if you let the pan heat up a lot before you add the veggies and eggs it makes easier to clean it." Mom explained.

I laughed, as grandma had said the same thing to me when she first started showing me how to make omelets. She also told me how mom had done a number on one of grandma's pan when she was younger and wasn't allowed to use it for weeks.

"Grandma taught me that seasoning the pan after you wipe it out is one of the most important things and I never did that." Mom said.

I smiled at my mom and she smiled back. I really wanted

things to be ok with us. I was tired of arguing with her and being difficult.

"Mom, can I talk to you?" I felt so much guilt over disobeying her and grandma's rules. I figured the truth was better coming from me.

"Sure, Riley. What about?"

I figured I would cut to the chase. "I went back into the attic." I waited a second before continuing. Mom's face didn't show any emotion. *Man, this was tough.* "I was mad at you and felt I had the right to know what you're trying to hide from me, especially since it's about my own dad. A dad that I never knew and want to know about." I slowed down and caught my breath. I looked at her and she still didn't show any emotion.

"I know I was wrong and I should've listened to you and grandma, but I was just really curious and it got the best of me." There, I said it. I let out a huge sigh of relief. I felt like a huge weight was lifted off my shoulders. Now all I had to do was wait for her reaction and ultimately my punishment.

Mom took a deep breath and sighed. "Riley, I'm not surprised and was wondering when you were going to come clean with me. Your grandmother and I already knew you were rummaging around up there even after you got caught. You left the light on so many times. When I would come home at night, I would see the light on. I asked your grandmother about it and she said she hadn't been up there but she could hear you walking around when you thought she went to bed," Mom said with a little hint of aggravation, yet understanding.

She grabbed my hands and said, "Thank you for telling the truth. You'll be grounded for the next few weeks and I hope you will listen from now on."
"Ok. That's fair. As far as grounded, you mean, no hanging out with friends, no TV and no computer or iPad, right? Can I still play basketball or am I grounded from that too?"

I figured I would put it all out there just to make sure I knew what I was in for. I hadn't even told her I made the team yet.

"No friend's after school, no TV, computer or iPad unless it's for school and you may participate in basketball. Does that clear things up?" Mom asked.

"It does. I have something that I need to return to you. I should have given it to you when you first caught me." I said with much hesitation in my voice.

I ran upstairs, grabbed the letter that I had hidden in my grandmother's bible and ran back downstairs hoping she wouldn't be too angry at me.

"Here." I said as I handed her the letter. "This was in the box that I first took from the attic. I read it. It's from dad to you." Her eyes welled up with tears and a sigh escaped her lips.

"OH... I had completely forgotten about this." She said with such sadness.

"As part of deploying we always wrote a letter in case something ever happened."

"Did you write one for me or grandma when you went to Iraq when I was younger?"

"Yes. In fact, I did. I gave your grandmother a package that was supposed to only be opened if something happened to me." Mom explained. "Nothing ever happened so I shredded them when I came home."

"This letter here-" she couldn't stop the tears from flowing now-"is something I never wanted and refused to take it from your father when he brought it up in conversation. I found out later that he gave it to your grandmother instead. She gave it to me the morning I learned your dad had been killed in Iraq." Mom took a breath and started again.

"I never did have the courage to read it. Your father was everything to me. He was my first and last love. We met when I was 14 and it was love at first sight. It's been so hard without him and I've just tried to shut everything out."

She explained.

"Mom- you don't- "I let my voice trail off. I felt bad for bringing this sadness back into her life. I gave my mom a hug and we just sat there for a few minutes holding each other.

She was the first one to break the embrace. Slowly opening the letter, she started reading it. More tears flowed and a smile crossed her face. When she finished reading it, she looked up with a smile on her face. "This is so like your father. He was always one for grand gestures and emotional letters. He used to write me love letters and leave them in my locker." She started laughing. "One day he was writing one in English class and the teacher, I can't remember her name, caught him and made him read it in front of the entire class. I was bright red with embarrassment."

I passed her a napkin. "I know I'm in trouble and I shouldn't have disrespected you but can I ask you questions about dad?" I didn't want to push my luck but knew I didn't want to miss my chance to finally get some answers.

"Sure, go ahead. Take it easy as this whole honesty and sharing my history thing is new for me." She winked and smiled through her tear-filled eyes.

I found it ironic that we were kind of the same about being honest. But mom and I were back. My heart was so happy and I couldn't wait to ask all the questions that I had been wanting to ask for years.

"Why don't you like talking about him?" I figured I'd get it out in the open.

"It's painful. I thought I was going to spend the rest of my life with your dad and he died leaving me in shambles. I was very pregnant when the black sedans with the flags drove up to our home. I had to adjust to being a widow, new mom and hold it together career wise. It's hard reliving those memories; they were my dreams and I still think of them. You look so much like your father, Riley." She reached for her napkin and wiped the tears. I could tell she was having a tough time, so I decided to take a break in the conversation.

"Omelets are finished," I said as I dropped the eggs and veggies onto her plate. "Hopefully I make these as good as grandma does. I know I already have trouble with getting the cookies to taste just right.

Mom smiled through her tears, "The eggs are fantastic, Honey. You're really growing up, aren't you? How about after the start of your being grounded we take a walk up into the attic and start going through some of my things that are up there? It's been such a long time since I've really been up there that you probably know more of what's there than I do."

"Guess I do," I replied. "Now all I have to get right is listening to you and grandma." I couldn't help but grin because I was so excited that I could finally talk and joke with her again even if I was in trouble.

"I forgot to tell you something, Mom." I could tell she was bracing herself as her hands gripped her coffee mug a little more and her knuckles began to get whiter. "It's nothing bad. I made the basketball team. I don't know what position I'll be playing because I was vomiting and didn't take a good look at the roster. I will have to go and look again and talk to coach." I was so excited and so happy that my mom was the first person I told.

"That's awesome news," mom said almost squealing. "Let's celebrate, tonight with some of grandma's famous cookies and some ice cream."

"That sounds like an awesome idea. I love you, Mom." I had a few tears in my eyes. I was so happy and couldn't help it.

"I love you too, Riley!" She put down her coffee and held her arms open and motioned for me to come over and give her a hug. Mom always gives the best hugs. They're like bear hugs where you don't want to let go.

"I missed your hugs, Mom." I said to her in a small voice.

"And I missed giving them to you, sweetheart. You up for church or do you want to just stay in your PJ's all day?"

"It's 11:30. We still have time to get ready. I would like to hear what the pastor has to say today. I really like his series on love and relationships and am looking forward to it. I can be ready soon."

"Sounds great. I'll clean up while you get ready and meet you at the car." Mom said.

As I ran upstairs to take a quick shower, I decided to get my journal out and write a few sentences about what had just happened between us before forgetting. Having happy entries were more exciting for me as there haven't been many of them lately. My room was messy, but my journal was nowhere to be found. School was the last place that it was with me, so I reached in my bag; two notebooks and a pencil box. Huh, it was gone! *Awe man! Someone had to have taken it. But who? If someone read it, my social life would be over.* Guess I'll just have to wait until school on Monday

Chapter Ten

Panic hit me like a ton of bricks. I tried to think of who would want to take something out of my backpack. Maybe they didn't mean to. I tried to remember if I could have misplaced it and couldn't. I remembered that I had written in my journal just before school started the day before and in Mrs. Tanzy's class and knew I put it back in my bag as I left class. I thought back to that day. The air was crisp, but it was a clear day. I had had 15 minutes before the first bell rang so I sat on the brick steps and started to write. The counselor from my last school had told me writing my feelings down in a journal was a good way to help me deal with my emotions of being a military kid and moving so much. Writing was something that I loved to do so it seemed like an easy task. I was writing a lot of my thoughts down about Sebastian that day and what happened between the two of us. A few of my friends had walked by and asked what I was doing and I had blown them off. I couldn't see any of them taking my journal since I didn't want to seem childish. For the most part, everyone had been nice to me since I had moved here so I couldn't think of anyone who would have wanted to take it. Well, maybe there was one person who could have taken it. Joey! He was in the hallway when my vomiting started and was making fun of me. He made fun of me a few times since the beginning of the school year but what would he want with my journal? I hoped he didn't have anything to do with it or I'd be toast.

Maybe Chloe would be able to help me figure out who took it or what I could have done with it. I picked up the phone and dialed her.

"Hi, this is Riley. Is Chloe there? "I asked.

"Sorry, Riley. She isn't home. She is out with her Dad. I'll let her know you called." Her mother's voice was soft and it almost sounded like she was crying.

"Ok. Thank you, Ma'am? Are you ok?" I hesitantly asked.

"Yes, I am sweetie. I'll have her call you. Goodnight." And then the line went dead.

She wasn't convincing and I could tell she wanted to get off the phone. Normally, she will ask me how school or my mom is. I think it's funny how adults think that they can hide their emotions, but not from me and not from most kids I know that are my age. I wish adults would just be honest and say what's happening. For me, covering up things only makes things worse. I wonder what is up with Sasha's mom. Hopefully they aren't getting divorced. I grabbed my ball and figured I would go to the courts and try to make sense of my feelings there. I always felt better after a few hours of shooting around. I'd worry about other things later...

The ball felt amazing in my hands. It always did but tonight it was different. The sun was setting and there were only a few clouds in the sky. Nights like this reminded me of sitting on the beach out in California when my mom was stationed at Vandenberg Air Force Base. She was working for air missile support at the time and had to work a lot of weekends. My friend's family would let me tag along at the beach with them and we'd sometimes camp out there if it was a long weekend at the military campground. The nights were always crisp and the basketball court was usually empty and the leather always felt smooth across my fingertips as I let it go into the air.

Today was just like one of those nights. The air was crisp and the ball flew perfectly out of my hands ... "Swish!" I ran the full length of the court, working on ball control, and dribbling between my legs. Although point guard wasn't my position, I still wanted to keep my skills sharp and make sure I was ready for the coach to use me anywhere. As I was running toward the far end of the court, I saw a small figure sitting on the bench. The person had a bright blue sweatshirt with a huge rainbow on the back of it. I knew that sweatshirt anywhere. Chloe only wore it almost every day. Her mother had gotten it for her a few years ago and it was so soft inside even to this day.

"Chloe!" I hollered to her but she didn't hear me.

She must have her headphones on. "Chloe!" I tried one more time, shot the ball and headed over to see what was up with her.

When I reached her, I tapped her on the shoulder. She jumped but settled down pretty quickly when she saw who it was.

"Hey Riley!" Here voice was so soft that I had trouble hearing her. She rubbed her hand across her face and brushed away tears from her swollen eyes. She sniffled so loud that I almost blocked my ears.

I sat down next to her and put my arm around her. "Holy Cow! Everything ok? You look like a hot mess!"

"Ugg… I know! My parents are ..." she swallowed hard..."are getting a ...a divorce." She barely could get the words out of her mouth without more tears falling down her cheeks. "My dad took me out for ice cream and told me. I can't believe it..."

"I'm sorry." Moving closer, I put out my hand for her to grab. She put her hand in mine and smiled weakly. I wish things were different for her, but I knew they would never be the same. I had seen it so many times with my friends. I wish her parents would stay together but I doubted it, because military parents get divorced all the time. In my old school, my friend Timmy's dad started dating my friend Heather's mom while their spouses were deployed. It never made sense to me why they dated other people when they were already married. Isn't being married like dating for the rest of your life? Chloe's life was upside down and would be for a while.

"I had him drop me off at the courts after he told me. It's pretty final" she said angrily and let go of my hand. "They've already sat down with the base legal officer and worked out a parenting agreement, child support and who is going to live where." She stopped crying and seemed angry. Her eyes had glossed over and it was like she was almost a different person talking. Her face was a deep red. "I don't understand how they had all this figured out and I didn't even have a say in it or have any real idea that it was happening. They are so selfish."

Sometimes I felt a little older for my age. I understood adult issues more than anyone would give me credit.

"You'll get through this. Sebastian and I are here for you." I know these were meaningless words right now. My actions would have to show it. Chloe was crying again so I just sat there for a few minutes next to her making sure she knew that I was there by putting my arm around her. Her shoulders were moving up and down.

"Do you have to move off base?" I couldn't help my curiosity.

"No, I'll be living with my dad. Mom is moving out this weekend and heading to Teen Challenge somewhere near Boston. From what my dad said she has been using too much of the drugs that the doctor gave her to help her with my grandma's death. She's taking too many of them and now she's addicted." Chloe eyes welled up with tears again.

"Really?" I tried not to let my jaw drop to the floor. I would have never guess that Chloe's mom was doing drugs. Whenever I'd call to talk to Chloe she seemed sad but I never in a million years would I have thought she was doing THAT. I sat there with my eyes bugging out of my head- in complete shock.

"I never imagined my mom would do drugs." Chloe stopped crying. "At least she realizes she has a problem and is willing to get help, right? I just wish my Dad would give her another chance, but I can't blame him? He said he's had enough and just can't stay with her anymore. He says he doesn't love her."

I had the feeling she was looking at me to help her figure everything out.

"I know you're hurting and upset, but I think you're right! She'll get better and things will go back to somewhat normal." I tried to give her a little sense of hope even though her life seemed hopeless right now.

I stood up and put my hand out. She grabbed it and jumped up. "No point in staying here all night! My grandma is going to worry. Why don't you come home and have dinner with me?" I figured grandma wouldn't mind Chloe coming over and since I didn't have a cell phone to call, I decided to invite her.

"Thanks, Riley. That sounds good. I think I'll give my parents a call and check to see if it's ok. I know my mom wanted to talk to me too..." Her voice trailed off as she started to make the call.

I gave her some space and went to grab my ball and water bottle. I couldn't believe what was happening to my friend and her family. The good thing was her mom was getting the help she needed.

"All set. Mom will come get me after dinner and we'll talk then." She grabbed the ball from me and took a jump shot from the three-point line.

"Swish!" When all else fails, we still have basketball.

Chapter Eleven

Dinner went well. Grandma let Chloe and I eat on the porch as it was such a nice night out. She cornered me as Chloe was washing up and asked me what was going on. My mom had grounded me and told Grandma that I wasn't allowed to have friends over. I'm glad she was made an exception for Chloe staying for dinner.

"Chloe's parents are getting a divorce," I said quietly. "Her father told her tonight and her mom is going to talk to her tonight after dinner with us."

"Oh, that's sad. I will be praying for them." Grandma let out a huge sigh.

"I wish there was something I could do to make Chloe feel better, Grandma. I feel so bad for all of them." My shoulders felt so heavy as I thought of my friend's situation with her parents. I have had friends whose parents had gotten divorced and they were never the same.

"Just keep praying, Riley. God will work everything out in His time and in His own way." Grandma said as she gave me a hug.

Chloe came out of the bathroom and we grabbed our plates and went out on to the porch. Grandma's food always made me feel good, especially when I was sad. Her famous American chop suey was what she called, "comfort food." One thing I knew, Chloe and her family needed all the comfort they could get right now. I am sure this is not easy for any of them. We finished our dinner quickly. We made some small talk, I guess all the emotional conversations were over. It was starting to sink in for me that many things would change and I might lose my friend if she moved or if something changed too drastically for her family.

Chloe's mom pulled up soon after we finished dinner. "Thanks, Riley." Chloe gave me a quick hug and slipped down the stairs.

Before I could even say "Your welcome" she raced to the car. I'm sure she was anxious about meeting with her mom. *Who wouldn't be?* She was playing with her hair, so there was definitely a little bit of nervous behavior going on. Every time that I saw her thinking about something intensly or nervous about something she would put her hair up in a ponytail and then take it down. She would do this repeatedly until I would tell her to stop. Tonight, at dinner was no different, but I decided not to say something this time and let her keep playing with her hair. I waved to her and headed in to the house to wash up and get ready to do my homework and go to bed. This was a long and emotional day and I couldn't wait to hit my pillow and drift off to sleep.

*****

The attic still called to me. The musty smell of the old boxes and rotting wood drew me in and each night I lay awake trying to find time to get back up there. My life was so busy with basketball and school and friends that I never had any time to keep searching for answers about my Dad. Mom was still closed mouth about the situation even thought I had fessed up about searching through her stuff. I had been grounded for a week and had dish duty for a month. Neither one was horrible considering it could have been worse. I was still a little upset that we weren't talking a lot about my Dad but I was definitely more understanding as to why. I wish I knew more about him. I don't think my mom really understands what it's like to grow up without a father. It's horrible. *Today is Tuesday. I'll go up there Thursday after our game. Mom will be at work and grandma has bible study so I will have some time to myself. Awe man. I forgot to do my exercises.* I looked at the clock. 22:30 it read. I guess there is no time like the present.

I jumped out of bed and decided I should get started on the 25 push-ups and 50 sit-ups coach wanted us to do each night. My floor was cold even though the weather had been gorgeous out today but I had to get these exercises done and I didn't want to go all the way downstairs to the living room where the floor was warmer. *You need to just push through this Riley.*

Halfway through my push-ups, I heard creaking from the floor above me, and dropped to the floor. I laid quietly trying to figure out who would be up there. Neither my mom or grandma had come upstairs. I was so deep in thought that one of them could have passed by my room without my knowing but I doubt it since. I heard boxes moving around and then loud crash. I got up and started to run downstairs, practically tripping over my own two feet. *Wait!* I thought for a minute. *There's no way, I'm letting anyone get into my mother's stuff except for me. And what if it was just mom? I'm tough and can handle this.* I grabbed the bat out of the hallway closet and turned toward the attic door. The movement upstairs had stopped and I thought I could hear crying. I decided that I would just run up there and yell loud. That way, if it was a stranger I would wake everyone in the house. *Here is goes.* I took a deep breath and opened the attic door.

"AHHHHHHH! Whoever is up here, you need to show yourself now! The police will be here any minute!" Screaming at the top of my lungs as I raced up the stairs. I held the bat behind my shoulder ready to swing.

"Hey! Riley!!! It's just me, Chloe! Please don't swing that bat!" she just as loud as she jumped up with her hands up in the air.

"Chloe, what the heck are YOU doing here? Why are you in our attic hiding like a burglar?" I tried to sound nice but the adrenaline in my body was causing my mind and heart to race. I took a long deep breath and lowered the bat.

Chloe lowered her hands and gave me a look that said it all. Her eyes were bloodshot and she looked like she had been crying for days.

"I needed to get out of my house and I remember you telling me about your attic. I figured no one goes up there so I snuck in through an open downstairs window. Your house was pretty dark and everyone was in their rooms so it was easy." She looked so sad as she explained what she did. "I just wanted to be alone. The conversation with my mom was hard and she leaves tomorrow for Teen Challenge. I heard her and my Dad arguing again so I snuck out the door and came over here. Did you know that the tree by the attic window is pretty easy to climb and the window was unlocked?" she shrugged her shoulders and let out a sigh. Man, this stuff with her parents was really weighing her down. I looked at her and saw that she had already lost some weight. They blue sweatshirt that she wore all the time didn't fit as it normally did. She was almost drowning in it.

Just then mom and grandma came running up the stairs. Mom had a bat in her hand and grandma had her caste iron pan.

"Chloe, Riley?!?! What in God's name is going on here?" Grandma said in a loud and upsetting tone. Before we could even answer, she turned and walked downstairs. She did not seem happy and I figured she was probably going to put her pan back in the cupboard.

"Mrs. Reagan, it's my fault." Sasha said quietly. "I was upset and I came here to get away from my parents fighting."

"Ok. Go downstairs girls, and wait in the living room. The base police are only a few minutes out. We'll get this all sorted out, Chloe. I'll call your parents now." Mom gave us both stern looks and turned and walked downstairs. Her voice sounded a little frustrated but understanding. I had heard this voice many times, especially when I was in a bunch of trouble. The sirens of the base police were coming down the street. We both moved quickly and waited on the couch like mom had told us. Chloe hung her heard the entire time.

The police pulled up to the house with their sirens and lights flashing so brightly in the night's sky that it blinded me when I looked at it even with the shades drawn in the living room. I felt a surge of anxiety run through my body as grandma met them at the front door. They were out there for about ten minutes when the Sargent came in to talk to us.

"Girls, you gave everyone quiet a scare tonight. Chloe, I just talked to your parents and you are welcome to stay with the Reagans tonight. Your mom and dad will come and get you in the morning. Is that ok with you?" The Sargent seemed very nice and he looked genuinely concerned about Chloe.

"That's fine. Thank you. I'll stay here tonight." She said quietly.

"Alright then. I'll let both your parents know." He nodded to both of us and left the room.

As soon as he left, Chloe looked at me and said, "Are you okay with me staying here the night?" Her eyes opened wide and full of desperation.

My frustration with Chloe was a little high but it wasn't over the top. Why didn't she just call me and ask? Why did she have to scare the crap out of our whole family? I can't really understand what she is going through since my parents aren't going through a divorce, so I decided to just let it go and not share my real feelings with her.

"Chloe, I am fine with whatever. Maybe a night away from the yelling will help you." Opening my arms wide, I gave her a big hug and she collapsed crying in my arms.

"I'm sorry. I feel like such a mess. My life is turning upside down. My mom is leaving tomorrow and after that life will never be the same. She's sorry and wants to get better but I just don't understand why they have to move toward a divorce now? I am mad at my dad for giving up on her and I am mad at her for doing this to our family. Why? Why is this happening to me?" She bawled her eyes out in my arms.

"I don't know. I know that your parents love you and that it's a mess right now but God will fix it, Chloe.

Please just keep praying and don't lose hope!" I just wanted to reassure her with all my might that things would work out. I had my doubts in everything. Just then a voice interrupted my thoughts.

"Chloe and Riley, can you come outside, please. We need to talk to." Mom said with some firmness yet understanding in her voice.

One of the officers spoke up. "Chloe, you're out after curfew so I need to tell you that next time there will be consequences. We have been informed about what is going on in your home life and are going to show some leniency this time. I need to tell you that breaking curfew and breaking into someone's home can lead to some pretty serious consequences so next time you need to think before you act. The Sargent here said that you will be staying the night and that your parents will pick you up in the morning." The officer was very firm with Chloe and gave her a stern look.

"I understand, Officer. I won't do it again." Chloe a said barely above a whisper.

"Okay. If everyone is fine and on the same page, we'll leave you to it. Have a good night. And, Chloe... keep your head up kiddo! Things will get better." And with a wink and a nod he left us standing there just looking at each other. None of us moved for a few minutes.

"I wish there was something I could say to help you feel better, Chloe." My Grandmother broke the silence with her words. "I know from hearing your mom and dad's side of everything this is a tough situation and that the good thing is that your mother is getting help. I am praying for all of you. My daughter and I talked and our home is your home." She reached over and gave Chloe a huge hug.

"We love you, Chloe. Why don't you and Riley go upstairs and get settled in for the night." Mom's voice was soft and compassionate.

"She can sleep in my bed and I can sleep on the couch in my room." I said without hesitation. Mom had moved a little couch into my room last week in case I wanted to have a friend sleep over. I'm glad she did.

"Thank you all for being so nice to me." Chloe said, her eyes swelling up with tears.

"No problem." We all said together and smiled at the same time.

As Chloe and I walked up the stairs, I thought that even though this night started off a little scary with lots of tears it was something that we would all figure out together. God is going to work all of this out, it's just a matter of time. I just hoped that Chloe would believe this as well. Tomorrow is another day and hopefully a better one.

*****

Kids were staring at Chloe and me as we were dropped off at school. I am not going to lie, I was a little uncomfortable because I didn't know why. Sebastian met us at the front door. He was sitting on the steps with an almost frantic look on his face. We dropped our bags and sat down next to him.

"It is all over the school and the base. I'm so sorry about your mom and dad." His eyes were wide with awe as he gave Chloe a big hug and didn't hesitate to glare at people as they stared at her. It was a small base so everyone talks. *Man, I hate the rumor mill!*

"I know people are talking but if anyone gives you a hard time, let me know and I'll take care of it. You're my friend and that's that!" From the stern sound in his voice, I knew he meant it.

"Thanks, Sebastian." Chloe already looked so uncomfortable, playing with her hair, and trying to avoid eye contact with anyone that would look at her. "People were texting me all night and I'm sorry, Riley if it kept you up! I ended up putting it on silent because people wanted to know what was going on."

Changing the topic, I asked "What is everyone doing after school today? The team doesn't have practice tonight so why don't you both come over and hang at my house. My mom has dropped me from being grounded. She left me a note this morning. We are doing better, and I guess I am back in her good graces and not grounded for weeks. Grandma can be talked into making some of her famous chocolate chip cookies." I need some time to have some fun and just relax with friends, away from the drama of everyone's lives. "There's a carnival on base this weekend if anyone wants to go too. My mom already said that I can go with a group of people. She'll be at work so she won't be there. Grandma will be working the church bake sale there both days."

"Both sound good to me! I just should check with my parents. I don't think we have anything planned." Sebastian said with eagerness in his voice. I really hoped he just wanted to hang out as friends this weekend because I didn't want to deal with boy drama right now. He didn't wink so that was a good thing.

"Let me check with my dad. I like the idea of coming over after school. I'd like to avoid my house altogether today if I can." Chloe's voice was so sad when she talked. She reached into her bag and grabbed her cell phone and started texting. "I think I want to go to the fair with my Dad. It's kind of been our thing for the past few years. He takes me on the ferris wheel and tries to win me the biggest bear he can."

The bell rang and we all jumped up and grabbed our backpacks.

"I'll see you both at lunch then," I said standing up.

"Later." Chloe said and walked off to her first class.

Sebastian lightly touch my arm as I walked by him. "Hey Riley. Can we talk sometime? Please I really need to talk to you." His voice was so serious and deep. I never hear him talk like this.

"Sure, how about at the carnival this weekend? Is everything ok?" As much as I didn't want to deal with drama, especially boy drama, he seemed determined to have a conversation.

"Yes and no. It's about you and me. I think we need to talk." He said with a hint of a question in his voice.

"I agree with you. I have been so busy with everything going on with Chloe that it kind of went on the back burner. We'll talk later." I gave his arm a quick squeeze and headed off to class. I had to walk away. I felt so overwhelmed with life in general. I felt like I was going to explode with all my thoughts in my head. My first class was study hall and I thought I should do some writing. That always seemed to help. I reached in my bag to grab my journal and then remembered that I didn't know where it was. *Man, could my life get any more complicated.* I tried to keep the tears from flowing but decided to duck into the bathroom and let them fall for a minute. The second bell rang and I washed my face off and dried it. *You got this, Riley! Get a hold of yourself.* I decided I would ask mom to take the day from school tomorrow. I would miss basketball, but I really needed a day to get a hold of all my feelings. She and I were on good terms now so I think she will be understanding. One of the things that she taught me in life is that I need to take care of myself even at a young age. Little did I know that it would be one of the best decisions I had made in a long time.

Chapter Twelve

Chloe and Sebastian were right on time after school. It was a beautiful day. Cookies at my house and then we went to the courts to shoot a round. I loved having the ball in my hand. The leather always made me feel like I was in control of my own destiny. Weird, I know. Chloe told me at lunch that she was going to go home first and see if her dad would let her come over first before heading over. He must have said yes as she showed up. I decided not to ask her about any conversations she was having with her parents and let her bring it up on her own. I tried not to think about the fact that Sebastian and I were going to "talk" on Saturday at the carnival. Earlier I had watched Sebastian and Sasha laughing as they walked up to my doorstep and I felt a twinge of jealousy and quietly gasped. They were both my friends and clearly there was nothing going on between the two of them. I knew I had nothing to worry about but I still had these feelings that I couldn't shake. I grabbed the ball after Sebastian missed a shot and started to dribble it over and over. *I wish things were simple in my life, God. Why do I always feel the need to help people and what are these feelings that I'm having toward Sebastian?*

I felt my arm jolt a little. "Hey! Riley, what's up with you? Are you going to shoot the ball or what?" Sasha was standing next to me and was giving me a weird look.

"Yea sorry. Hey guys, I don't think I am up for playing ball. I don't feel too good. I think I ate too many cookies. I'm going to walk home. Call me later, Chloe?"

Sebastian gave me a quizzical look and I just shrugged. "You ok?"

"Yea, I'm ok. I'll see you guys tomorrow. Have fun. And don't worry I'll be all right." I tried to put a smile on my face but I was too confused and emotional. I just wanted to go home and cozy up in my bed.

As I walked away, I saw them starting a game of one on one as Chloe was checking the ball to Sebastian.

Good. At least they weren't just sitting around talking about me. The walk home seemed to take a long time even though my house was just around the corner from the park. I only had a few things for homework so I decided it could wait and would go straight to my room when I got home. I noticed my grandmother's car wasn't in the driveway. She must have gone out for a minute. I left her a note on the kitchen counter telling her I was home from the courts and would be taking a nap and went upstairs to my room. It was still warm from the sun shining in it all day but I felt like I needed to get under the covers. I was freezing. I closed my eyes and felt my eyelids get heavy. I felt like I could sleep for days. It was only just a few days ago that I went home with the flu. Maybe this was just left over...

The next think I knew, I felt someone nudging me and I opened my eyes. I felt hot and sweaty and completely miserable. "Riley? Hey Riley! Wake up sweetheart." I looked up and saw my mom and grandmother standing over me.

I rubbed my eyes and looked at the clock… 22:30. "What? I slept so long!" I couldn't believe it. I must have fallen asleep mid thought.

"You slept right through dinner. Grandma called me after you didn't come down for dinner and we have been checking on you every hour to make sure you were ok. You had a temperature of 103 degrees and were talking in your sleep a lot. Do you remember me giving you Tylenol a few hours ago? How do you feel now?" She grabbed the thermometer and took my temperature. "98.9," she said as she let out a huge sigh of relief. I couldn't even answer any of the questions that she asked me.

"Your temperature is down which is a good sign. When was it that you started to feel poorly, sweetheart?" My grandmother asked.

"I was playing basketball and suddenly felt really tired, exhausted and emotional. I left the courts and went straight to bed. Next thing I know, you're waking me up." I decided to leave out the part that I was an emotional mess right now with everything going on. "I'm tired but a little hungry. Is there anything left from dinner?" I looked at grandma who already had begun walking to the door.

"I'll fix you some soup, dear. I'll have it ready in a moment. Come down when you're ready." Her smile was soft as she walked to the door. Man, I love grandma…. Always knowing what I need and being right there when I need it.

"Sebastian and Chloe both called. They were worried about you." My mom explained.

I rolled my eyes and she caught it. She gave me the look that only mothers can give when they want you to cough up information.

"I'm struggling mom. Moving here has been tough and everyone I know is having relationship problems and now there is this "thing" with Sebastian. I miss my friends from back home and I just don't feel like myself." I started crying and just let the tears flow. *Wow, it felt good to let it all out.*

"Riley, you don't need to help everyone. You are just a kid and only one person. I know this move has been hard for you but take it one day at a time. You're not going to settle in all in one day or even just a few weeks. Change takes time." Mom was right and her voice was very sincere.

"What do I do about Sebastian, Mom? I like him but I don't want to lose him as a friend. He wants to talk to me at the carnival this weekend." I kept sniffling and Mom handed me a tissue.

"Well…" mom hesitated for a moment… "You could hear him out. I think you are still too young for dating and already have a lot going on with school and basketball." Mom was playing with the tissue box and I could tell that she was not comfortable with this conversation.

"Didn't you meet Dad when you were just a little older than me?" I wasn't sure if I should ask that question but I did, anyways.

"Yes, I did and we decided to stay friends first. After we had figured out that we had feelings for each other we decided to get to know each other before we thought about dating. Plus, my father would not let me date, especially someone who was older than me." I loved when my mom talked about when she was young. It made me feel that she knew what I was going through.

"Should I do the same thing with Sebastian? What if he wants to be more than friends and I am not ready? What do I do then? I barely even know him." My mouth just kept spitting off more and more questions and I started to cry again.

"Riley, it's ok. You don't have to decide right away if you want to marry him or not" Mom had a huge smile on her face but I seemed to miss it.

"Wait! What? Marry him? Mom what are you…" It was then that I saw the smirk on her face. "Ha-ha… you're funny, Mom!" I playfully tried to punch her in the shoulder. She really knew how to make me feel better.

"You're thinking into this too much. Go and have a talk with Sebastian. Tell him how you feel and don't worry about it so much. Worst case scenario tell him I told you that you can't date yet. In my opinion, I think you are way too young to date anyways." I could tell she was a little worried about me since she was reassuring me over and over not to worry so much. And to be honest, it was comforting knowing my mom didn't want me to date just yet.

"Sounds good, Mom. Thank you for letting me talk and cry all over you. Want to get something to eat with me?" I was so hungry and was secretly hoping that grandma was cooking some homemade chicken noodle soup. I know she kept some frozen in the freezer.

"Food sounds great. I didn't eat dinner yet. It was a long day and I was stuck at the hanger later than I thought I would be. I am going to have you stay home with Grandma tomorrow just to make sure that this isn't the flu bug that you had a last week. I think you are just run down and need some rest." Just then did I realize that mom was still in her uniform and it was almost 2300. Maybe this move was harder on her than it was on me. She didn't work this late all the time at our last base.

"Mom, I love you." I said giving her a hug.

"I love you, too, sweetheart." She said giving me a huge squeeze back. I love my mom's hugs. We called them "bear hugs." When she squeezed me tight back I could feel every part of her body giving me a hug. I felt so safe and like I didn't have a care in the world.

"Now, let's go get some food." She said with a smile and jumped up toward the door.

I grabbed my bathrobe and took off my basketball shoes that I was still wearing. I rolled my eyes while taking them off. *Man, I must have been out of it if I wore these to bed.* Mom was right. I needed to stop overthinking this thing with Sebastian. He was my friend and that was that.

Chapter Thirteen

I spent all day Wednesday at home relaxing under the watchful eye of my 72-year-old grandmother. She kept taking my temperature repeatedly and asking me if I needed anything. It was great but almost to the point of annoying. I felt much better. The night before mom and I had a bowl of chicken noodle soup and a grilled cheese sandwich and talked for a litter while longer. She was beat and had to be back to her squadron at 0530 for PT so she wanted to get some sleep. I, on the other hand spent my day watching TV, reading my Nancy Drew book on the porch and drinking tea.

Now, I was back at school and ready to face all my issues with Sebastian. As I walked up to the school steps I was nervous but excited at the same time. I was determined to make the most of my day and to stop letting my emotions run my life. The first person I saw was, Joey. *God, you must be kidding me! Of ALL people to run into.* I barely know him but he is so mean to me and the one I thought took my journal. I didn't have the courage to confront him just yet. I heard he made fun of a heavier girl, in the front of the whole cafeteria, because she had a plate of fried food. I was told the girl wouldn't go to the cafeteria for weeks because she was so embarrassed for being called "a fatty!" I have had some run-ins with him but they've been very petty. I had it easy but I had the sinking feeling that I was in his line of fire. He was the school bully and if you were in his crosshairs, you were toast. I took a big gulp. He was holding something in his hand, which caught me by surprise and caused me to stop in my tracks.

"Hey, Riley, I think this belongs to you." He said with a wide and almost evil looking grin. The sides of his lips curled a little and he winked at me as he reached toward me.

"It does, how did you get it?" I grabbed my journal and tucked it safely into my backpack. I was trying not to be rude but this kid was such a pain to deal with.

"It dropped out of your bag when Mr. Connell was helping you when you got sick. I grabbed it but you were already gone so I couldn't get it back to you and had to get to class." He seemed to have an answer for everything. I had been in school most of this week and he could have gotten it back to me. Why did he hold out? Oh, no, maybe he read it.

"Did you read it?" I asked with a hint of anger in my voice. I was trying to cover up my feelings of dread.

"No... I would never do that. It's your journal and your private thoughts about people. Why would I do that?" He said it with a lot of sarcasm and I didn't believe him. Of course, he read it. "Thanks for returning it." I tried to be sincere but I knew something bad was going to happen if he was being this way or at least that's what I thought.

"No problem, Riley. And hey... you should really try and write for the school newspaper. You are a GREAT writer. I'm pretty sure Sebastian will think you are a good writer too." He laughed an evil laugh, made kissy faces, and walked away giving me a wink. My heart sunk. Oh, crap! He did read it. I wanted to chase him and yell at him but I kept my cool and just watched him walk away. What was the verse about praying for your enemies that my mother talked to me about? I didn't want to pray for him right now. What I really wanted was for him to trip and fall on his face and everyone to laugh at him. Wait, I really shouldn't think this way. I needed to treat him like I wanted to be treated and take the high road.

The bell rang, and it brought me back to reality. I had to get to homeroom before the second bell. Good thing it was right around the corner. I had to let everything with Joey go, for right now. Sebastian smiled at me as I started to walk into homeroom. Instantly my face turned a deep red as I smiled back. Oh boy, I am so glad I can escape into class.

The rest of the day and week for that matter was uneventful. The base carnival was postponed until the next week since it was pouring. Chloe was hanging out more with her dad after school as they got used to their "new normal" without her mom in her life. She told me that everything went well with her transitioning into Teen Challenge. She already written her a letter where she apologized about her actions and ruining the family. Basketball was in full force and I was practicing all the time. If I wasn't in the school gym, I was at the courts down the street or my house. Sebastian would join me sometime. We still hadn't talked but decided that the carnival would be the best time to talk since it would be a fun and light atmosphere.

*****

My life seemed to be going very well. I had gotten myself back in the groove of waking up early, doing my devotion and writing in my journal. Running and ridding my bike down at the canal because a huge part of my

schedule as it was so relaxing. The wind would sometimes

pick up which made it hard to ride but it was good workout.

Sometimes when I would sit on the jetty and think about

how people didn't believe in God with all the beauty

surrounding them. The seagulls that flew around me and

the way the sun set over the water was so amazing that it

made me love where I live even more.

It was the Friday before the carnival, and while

walking to school, the preparations for my talk with

Sebastian were already taking place in my head. I had

already talked about it with Chloe and she said we should

be friends first and then maybe date later in life. Entering

the school, I stopped dead in my tracks. There were papers

everywhere and tons of kids were staring at me. Grabbing

one of them, I saw that it was one of the entries to my

journal. My face turned bright purple as I contemplated

what to do. All I could do was just stand there, looking like an idiot as people laughed and pointed at me. *Is this what it feels like to be completely humiliated? Why would Joey do this to me? What did I do to deserve this?* Suddenly, I felt the world becoming dark and the other kids becoming smaller. My body felt hot and cold and my world began to spin. Breathing became difficult as I frantically searched to grab something stable. Joey was standing there laughing while sarcastically calling me an awesome writer. Grabbing into the air, I latched onto the nearest person, Sebastian.

"Sebastian, please help…" I cried and everything went dark.

Waking up in the nurse's office was the next thing I knew. Sebastian sitting by the door.

"Hey, Riley. You're awake. Let me get the nurse." His voice was soft and he sounded concerned.

The nurse came in and smiled. "You gave us quiet a scare young lady. Passing out like that in the middle of the hallway. How do you feel now?"

"I feel a little shaky but other than that I feel ok." Speaking quietly. I sat up and drank the juice she offered me. "Do I have to go to class today or can I go home?"

"Your Mom is on her way. She is going to take you to the doctor." The nurse explained. Sebastian made his way across the room and stood by my side and I have to admit I didn't mind. "Sebastian, you should get to class. I'll be right back with a pass for you to give to your teacher."

As the nurse walked away, Sebastian reached for my hand. I looked up at him and his eyes said it all. "Sebastian, those papers all over the school..." Taking a deep breath..."they are about you. Joey stole my journal... he photocopied it and hung them up everywhere. I was so embarrassed and overwhelmed. Now the WHOLE school knows my personal feelings about so many things." I knew

I was laying on the dramatics, but I really was upset about all of this.

"Phew... Ok... that makes sense. I was worried that something was wrong with you. I would have probably passed out too if someone knew my inner thoughts about you" Sebastian said with a soft smile and a sigh of relief. "Don't worry about it, kid! Joey is a bully and he is known for picking on the new kid! It will blow over soon." His voice was a little shaky but I could tell he was trying to be genuine.

"My mom is going to be here soon and you should get back to class. I'm not sure about going to the carnival this weekend. Showing my face in front of everyone is something that doesn't sound like fun right now," I said to Sebastian. People will probably be laughing at me for months. My hair was so sweaty and I was a hot mess. One good thing is that my clothes were comfortable and that gave me some comfort. Basketball practice was right after school so sweats were on the agenda today.

"Riley, don't worry about it, there will be other carnivals. I just want to say that I like having you as my friend. If I'm completely honest, I guess I really don't know you that well…" He was saying everything so fast that I could barely keep up. He reached for my hand again. His was sweaty and he was shaking a little bit.

"I like you, Riley. There it is, I said it. It is now out in the open. I really like you and want to be more than friends but don't want to lose you as my friend." His face was beet red and so was mine. I'm sure mine was purple. My heart was beating so fast. *Sebastian Cook likes ME!*

"Oh Sebastian, I like you too." Quietly whispering and not believing the words that were coming out of my mouth. I had so many thoughts running through my head and just wanted to kiss him. Should I tell him I want to be just friends? Or should we start dating? This is so confusing. *Why is being honest so hard? What if he gets mad and decides he doesn't like me anymore?*

"Sebastian, I want to be more than friends too but I think we should get to know each other a little better. I'm scared. My mom does not want me to date yet. I mean, seriously Sebastian, we are only in the 8th grade. I have school and basketball and a new life to get used to. Can we just be friends and get to know each other?" I didn't want to sound like I was giving too many excuses. Maybe one day we would be girlfriend and boyfriend but not right now. Looks like I just talked myself into a decision. That wasn't as hard as I thought it was going to be. Plus I didn't know much about his personal life and his beliefs and that was huge in my book.

"I get it, Riley. You don't have to explain." He looked defeated and relieved at the same time. He started to pull his had away but then he stopped and held it tighter.

He looked me in the eyes, bent down and gave me a kiss on the forehead. It made me feel so special.

"Get better, Riley. And don't worry about us. We'll be just fine." He gave me a hug and then slipped away out the door.

I didn't know what to think. Was he mad? He said he got it but did he really understand? And the kiss he gave me. What did it mean? Wow, Riley! Here you go again! Working yourself up again. I heard my own voice and realized I was saying these things aloud. Sebastian agreed to be friends and to get to know each other and that was it. He liked me and wanted to still be friends.

I laid back and closed my eyes. The beds in the nurse's office were not comfortable at all. They were stiff and felt like they were made of plastic. *I can't wait to get out of here and just go home.* I was looking forward to the carnival this weekend but with everyone in the school knowing my feelings about Sebastian and everything else, there was no way I could show my face. I heard the nurse in the background talking to someone. I knew that voice anywhere. It was my mom's. She sounded upset and worried. Her tone was even but it was raised so I knew someone was going to get a stern talking to and I hoped it wasn't me.

Just then the nurse, principal and my mom came into the bed area.

"Hey sweetheart!" My mom's face was beet red and she ran over to me. "I am so sorry that this happened to you. How do you feel?" She was feeling my forehead and rubbing my arm.

"I'm ok, Mom. Seriously. I was upset and there are papers all over the hall from my journal. Joey stole my journal and copied pages out of it. I was so upset that I passed out. Really, I'm fine. Sebastian said that this isn't

his first time completely humiliating a new student." I tried
to reassure her but I don't think it worked.

"That's horrible! Principal Denaro, what is going to
be done about this nonsensical bullying of my daughter?
This Joey boy will not get away with this." Her voice
sounded angry and her hand was tightening on my wrist. I
pulled it away slowly and started to get up and grab my
things.

"We will look into the incident, Ms. Tanner. I can
assure you that this is a bull- free school and we take this
thing very seriously!" He didn't look happy, especially
when my mom was scolding him and using the voice she
uses on me when I get in trouble.

"Apparently, Joey doesn't understand that bullying
is not allowed here. This is not the first time he targeted my
daughter and now he has humiliated her in front of the
entire school. I'm taking Riley to the doctor and I expect a

full report by the end of the day. Thank you and good day."
And with that she took my hand and led me out of the
nurse's office. I was proud of mom. She stood up for me
and wanted answers from the principal. Hopefully he can
deliver. Thankfully the halls were empty when we walked
out of school. I couldn't believe it. I was finally out of
there. *Now I can breathe.*

"Mom, can we move? I don't want to go back to
that school ever again!" I gave her the saddest look that I
could manage.

"Oh gosh, sweetie... this will blow over. I promise it
will. It just might take some time." She sounded tired. Her
voice was soft and a little raspy. "Let's get you to the
doctor and make sure that you're ok, just in case. Then I get
you home for some relaxation." I nodded to her in
agreement.

"The nurse told me that Sebastian carried you in his arms into her office and was like your knight in shining armor!" Her voice was filled with playful sarcasm.

"Yes, he did. He was so sweet and caring and even gave me a kiss on the forehead. We decided that we're going to be friends." I left out the part where he professed that he likes me. *I don't have to tell her everything.* "We talked a little and then he had to go to class but we're going to get to know each other and just stay friends for now." I was happy with that decision.

"That's good to hear. I think it's best you get to know each other before anything else. It is good to have a strong friendship before dating someone. Is Sebastian a Christian or believe in God?" Mom's face showed some concern when I shrugged my shoulders.

"I don't know much about his personal life. I know a little about his family but other than that we play basketball and talk about school stuff." It made me a little nervous that I didn't know much about him but I shrugged it off since I was going to find out about all of it soon enough.

"At least you two have a plan and it seems like a good one. I'd like you to stay close to home this weekend and not go to the carnival even if the doctor gives you a clean bill of health."

"I'll stay close to home, I promise. From what I heard in the doctor's office, the carnival might be canceled due to the weather." And with that, I hopped into the car. The seat was a little warm but at least it wasn't cold, that kind of weather was on its way I am sure. Mom turned on the radio and we both started singing to Carrie's song "Jesus take the Wheel!" No matter what happened, I knew I could always count on mom.

*****

After we got home from the doctor, mom said she had to go back to work. My doctor gave me a clean bill of health and ordered me to rest this weekend. Going to school on Monday gave me butterflies in the pit of my stomach and not to mention that the carnival was this weekend. I decided to just stay at home and listen to my doctor. Since we had moved here, I spent my days trying to fit in at school and doing my best to help people fix their problems and it was stressing me out. The base doctor told my mom that she thinks that I need to talk to a counselor or therapist and find a good way of coping with my stress. Not a fan of the idea but my mom said she would consider it and we would talk about it later. Things were so much simpler before we moved here. I left my room and went down to see what was for breakfast.

"Ring." Great! I bet its mom. I rolled my eyes as I picked up the phone.

"Hello, Riley speaking." I said in my most upbeat voice.

"Hey, Riley. It's Joey." His voice sounded almost robotic.

"What do you want?" I was startled by my own voice. I sounded angry.

"I just wanted to say…" He started to say in a quiet voice but I cut him off before he could finish.

"You wanted to say what? How sorry you are for ruining my life? For humiliating me in front of the whole school by sharing my most inner thoughts with everyone? Is that what you want to say? Huh?" I was shouting at him. My fists were bawled up and I was crying.

"No. I was going to say. Good luck in school on Monday." He broke out in laughter. His voice was like nails on a chalkboard. I was so angry that I screamed at him even louder.

"Don't call me again. You hear me! I don't know how you even got my number but leave me alone!" And with that, I slammed down the phone and ran into the kitchen. Tears were flowing and I put my head down on the counter. I couldn't do this anymore. Why did Joey have to be so mean? What did I ever do to him?

"Ring." I looked into the living room and glared at the phone. I ran over to it, picked it up and started yelling right away.

"Joey, I told you to stop calling me. I mean it. Stop bullying me NOW!" I was just about to hang up the phone when I heard a different voice on the line.

"Riley, sweetheart, what's wrong?" I gasped since I didn't think my mom would be calling. Oh no!

"I'm sorry Mom. I thought you were Joey! He called me and I flipped out on him!" I had calmed down a little but my heart was still racing. I didn't want mom to go crazy on the principal or Joey's parents for that matter, especially since Joey's dad outranked my Mom. I didn't want her to get in any trouble for being insubordinate.

"I will be calling the principal and setting up a meeting first thing Monday morning. I have had it with this boy bullying you. It is not right or healthy for you." When mom set her mind to do something she made sure she got it done. I hoped the meeting would go well and hoped that I didn't have to be there for it. It would be embarrassing enough just to go to school on Monday morning.

"Mom, I can handle it." I tried to make a final plea for me to take care of it, but I already knew it wouldn't work.

"Riley, you are bright, caring, and strong girl who doesn't deserve to be bullied in school. It's my job as your mother to take care of these kind of things especially when you have done what you can on your end. Don't worry, I'll be professional with Joey's parents. I understand your concern and I know who his parents are." She was laughing now. "Can you imagine what Joey would do if he was in my squadron? Hopefully, this young boy can get his act together and stop this destructive behavior." Mom was right. She would be better at handling this than me.

"Thanks, Mom. You're the best. I'm going to take a shower and work on some homework that's due next week."

"Ok, sweetheart. I love you. Make sure you take it easy. I'll be home for dessert."

Mom hung up first and I was left there holding on to the phone. I just stood there for a few minutes wondering why life could be so hard and complicated. Hopefully, things can just get easier. If this is what eighth grade was like, I can only imagine what high school will be like. And with that final thought I put the phone down on the receiver and went to my bedroom to do my homework. When I got to my room, I saw my mother's journal on my bed with an envelope addressed to me from Dad. *What was this? Was this what I think it was? A letter from my Dad?*

To be continued…